Decima Blake, aged thirty-two, has a long-standing interest in child protection. Having worked with teenagers, she is deeply passionate about child victims of crime. In writing *Hingston's Box*, Decima drew on her love of classic English murder mysteries and ghost stories. Her interest in English Literature was ignited by two highly motivational teachers who made her A Level studies enjoyable, character forming and invaluable to her future endeavours.

Hingston's Box raises awareness of the vulnerability of all children to exploitation. A percentage of royalties will be donated to the charity Embrace Child Victims of Crime.

HINGSTON'S BOX

Decima Blake

HINGSTON'S BOX

Vanguard Press

VANGUARD PAPERBACK

© Copyright 2016
Decima Blake

Photography Seamus Ryan

A CIP catalogue record for this title is
available from the British Library.

ISBN 978 1 784651 54 1

*This is a work of fiction. Names, characters, businesses, places, events and
incidents are either the products of the author's imagination or used in a
fictitious manner. Any resemblance to actual persons, living or dead, or
actual events is purely coincidental.*

*Vanguard Press is an imprint of
Pegasus Elliot MacKenzie Publishers Ltd.*
www.pegasuspublishers.com

First Published in 2016

**Vanguard Press
Sheraton House Castle Park
Cambridge England**

Printed & Bound in Great Britain

In recognition of all who strive to protect children from becoming victims of crime.

Chapter One
Twenty-seven Days

'The bullets in this jar…' he balanced the vessel between his thumb and forefinger, 'were taken from the body of murdered Constable Choat.' Standing tall, Detective Sergeant Jason Hingston scanned the audience, his eyes revealing the compassion that his trained voice disguised.

The members of the Metropolitan Police History Society, largely male and mature in service, sat forward in their seats. Their faces were solemn as they hung onto the words of Hingston, the youngest Society member, aged thirty-two.

Hingston continued. 'This jar, is one of over a dozen of its kind. You will see them later tonight in the Houndsditch murders collection on display in the museum downstairs.'

A round of applause followed and the Chair of the History Society, a white-haired, retired Chief Superintendent named Fynn Mannix, walked onto the stage. 'Thank you, Jason, for a fascinating talk which has given us much to reflect upon. The bravery of the three City of London police officers who lost their lives and the two who suffered life-changing injuries must not be forgotten. A few months past the centenary anniversary adds great poignancy and is, of course, the reason why the City of London Police have allowed us to use their premises this evening.'

Hingston nodded, smiled and stepped down from the stage.

Mannix turned to the audience. 'Before I introduce our next speaker, I'm delighted and *relieved* to advise that the historian who will be showing us around the museum has finally arrived!'

'You told her this station is unrecognisable from its days as a Roman barracks?' Hingston called to Mannix with a wide smile, a short distance from his seat within the audience. His brown eyes glinted.

A few laughs and a boisterous cheer died down, allowing Mannix to continue. 'Jason, you're athletic and as you're on your feet, could you bring her up from Reception?'

'Sure,' said Hingston.

Mannix began to introduce the next talk.

World War Two was Hingston's favourite period and so he sped out of the Wakefield Mess to ensure a prompt return.

Ten minutes later, Mannix received a call. The historian was still waiting in Reception. Concerned by Hingston's absence, he went to investigate.

Down the marble staircase Mannix hurried; past the enormous trophy cabinet and the baby grand piano. His feet tapped increasingly faster on the stairs and the police station fell quieter with each floor he descended. The May evening sunshine maintained a restful ambience in the station.

On the ground floor, off a dark, narrow corridor, Mannix reached the integral door labelled "Museum". The door was ajar and conservation lighting glowed through the crack. As he leant towards it to enter, he noticed his reflection in the glass pane, behind which a plethora of police helmet badges were displayed regimentally. A powerful floral scent made him stop and look over his shoulder. The corridor was still. He inhaled, but the fragrance had dissipated.

Frowning, he pushed the door open. It did not make a sound. Two eyeless mannequins in uniform stood guard aside the glass cabinets that were filled with equipment, clothing, medals and criminal artefacts collected over a period of one hundred and eighty years.

Mannix breathed silently as his vision adjusted to the yellow lighting, reflective glass and the multitude of faces that were photographically preserved behind it; police officers, criminals and the post mortem images of the Houndsditch murder victims.

He walked between the cabinets and saw the outline of a tall person slumped on the opposite side of the central display case. 'Jason?' Mannix called and quickened his pace. Mannix crouched next to him.

Hingston's eyes were staring straight ahead, focused on nothing distinguishable. His downturned mouth was clamped into place by his clenched teeth and his neck muscles were tense. His mid-brown hair was roughed up. Dried tears had left streaks down his slim cheeks and his eyes were still moist.

'Jason!' repeated Mannix.

Hingston blinked once. His head jolted toward Mannix like a mechanical toy springing into action. His brown eyes appeared alive again and after giving a look of realisation, concern flooded his face. He opened his mouth, then paused. 'I can't catch him... I can't,' Hingston whispered.

'What's happened to you?' Mannix muttered as he reached for his mobile phone and dialled. 'Get me a first aider. Museum. Now!'

* * *

Like a miniature searchlight, the sun reflected off the rim of the mug which stood squat and stubbornly amongst an array of police paraphernalia. A decade of slogans and acronyms decorated random stationery and knickknacks. A collection of well-thumbed files lay scattered across the desk. The mug itself, labelled "Best Detective" remained full of cold coffee.

He pictured Daniel and Nathan Clarke, the fifteen-year-old twins who had left school and disappeared: the absence of any trace on CCTV; the silence of their peers; their parents who had become despondent and abject; their siblings, Robert and Alice, thirteen and nine, who were caught in the pain and uncertainty. At three forty-five p.m. in broad daylight, someone should have seen something that would provide a lead.

He stared at his framed commendation awarded to Detective Constable Jason Hingston on the 19th of September 2008 and read the accolade: "for dedication and investigative excellence throughout Operation SEMAPHORE which resulted in the identification and conviction of four sex offenders". For a moment, his eyes closed.

'Sarge? Do you want another coffee?' a male voice called across the open plan office.

The brief release was over. 'No thanks, Rob. I'm just in the middle of something right now,' Hingston said. To the bottom right of his computer screen he caught sight of a meeting request. "DS Hingston 1:2:1, my office".

Before he could catch hold of the mouse the phone rang. 'Jason, I've just sent you an updated meeting request. How are you fixed for ten thirty?' Detective Inspector Brace was, in Hingston's opinion, a control freak; highly competent, but very demanding. In tune with her usual management style, she had moved the appointment forward by half an hour and "how are you fixed" meant "make yourself available – now".

Before the call ended, Hingston had formed a series of loops along the telephone cord, pressing down so hard that over half his thumbnail was almost totally white.

* * *

'Jason, I take it this meeting has not come as a surprise to you?'
Brace did not smile. She eyeballed Hingston and gestured to him to
take a seat.

'No, ma'am.' His hands were warming, becoming
uncharacteristically sticky and the strumming of anxiety in his
chest had returned full force.

'I've received the report from Occupational Health.'

'Ma'am, if I may interject.'

'No. Jason, their recommendation stands. I happen to agree and
in a few weeks' time I am confident you will be back with the team
and more importantly, back to your usual self.'

'I don't need the time off; I can handle this case the same as any
other.'

'Jason, no one is saying that this case is the direct cause.
Granted, the change has occurred in under a month.'

'The Clarke twins disappeared on the fifteenth of April,'
Hingston said. 'It's been twenty-seven days. There's no reason why
the circumstances should be affecting me, my performance…'

'Jason, I have observed the change. It is obvious from simply
looking at you that you are not sleeping, let alone the associated
difficulties which the report touches on.'

Hingston blinked his bloodshot eyes and tried to relax his tense
shoulders. He knew what Brace was referring to: the shadows under
his eyes, his faded enthusiasm and the energy lost from his long
strides, which would normally carry him expeditiously wherever he
went. His hands were rested on his slim fit, charcoal grey trousers
but there was a mild blotchiness which had arisen just behind his
knuckles and extended back towards his wrists. He glanced at his
cufflinks and reminded himself that he did check his appearance
before leaving the house this morning; hair combed, parted off-

centre and a small amount of wax applied to the longer sections at the front; shirt and tie matching. Hingston complained inwardly and touched his cheek. 'Didn't shave.'

He stared at Brace who continued. 'If the Occupational Health assessment hadn't occurred as a result of last week's incident at your History Society meeting, I would have had no choice but to refer you. I am responsible for you. You have passed every mandatory assessment in the previous six years. You were promoted following Operation SEMAPHORE and your performance has continued to be consistently outstanding. It is the nature of the work of this unit that demands these assessments. It is not a failure. It is part of the job.' Brace sat upright at her desk which unlike Hingston's, was immaculate and displayed a large picture frame adorning a professional portrait of her two pedigree red setters. These russet dogs gazed serenely and piously across the office.

In a similar manner Brace fixed her eyes on Hingston. Her straight nose and angular blonde bob remained perfectly still as she continued. 'We all experience some of the trauma the families go through. Sexual offences, missing persons, child abuse. Over time it will have an effect. Now, I'd like you to collate the papers from your desk and I will hand the package over to Brian who will be dealing with the case in your absence.'

Hingston hesitated, considering whether to argue the point. The Police Federation had already been appraised and were supportive of the leave; there was no alternative arrangement. As Hingston's heart raced, he saw a flash of the open meadow and curly hair; a scene which first stole into his mind three weeks ago and since stalked his days and nights with an unwelcome familiarity. But where were the chimes? Those soft, peculiar chimes that without invitation or an explanation of their origin, had provided a soothing, musical antidote since his problems began. It was always the same few bars repeated over and over. They played out a moderate, simplistic tune which would rise and fall, and delicate glissandos embellished the gaps between the notes. He could not identify the music, but he had grown to yearn for its melody.

Without his calming chimes and sat before Brace, he questioned himself whether he had been too open in his Occupational Health assessment. To disguise the truth was against his nature. Indeed he is the finder of truth, or so he once thought. Deflated, he acknowledged Brace and dutifully returned to his desk.

* * *

"Best Detective". Hingston considered the words before upturning the cold contents down the sink. Consumed by the investigation he was about to lose, he ambled back to his desk. He picked up the statement of Robert Clarke. "I waited at the turning by Bishop's Avenue until four p.m. They were always there by this time, the latest. I rang Daniel first and then Nathan but they didn't answer. At 4.10 p.m., I called them again. Nathan's phone was off. Daniel's went to voicemail, so I left him a message to say I was going home and they better hurry up or Mum will be cross."

'Jason!' It was Brace, who had begun to shuffle the papers on his desk into neat piles. He had not noticed her approach. 'I asked you to collate, not read.'

'Sorry,' he began to feel like *he* was a teenager trying to avoid an adult's reprimand. 'Just sorting chronologically.' He knew that sounded as feeble as he felt. Annoyed and embarrassed he returned the statement to the top of a pile and swept the papers into a hefty bundle.

As he neatened the stack with the dexterity of a cardsharp, Brace raised her left eyebrow and gave a nod of approval, a small smile quickly fading as she met his tired eyes. 'Now, Jason, go and look after yourself.'

Hingston gave the bundle one firm tap on the desk. He inhaled deeply, lifted the papers and increased his grip, much as an officer may squeeze the upper arms of a dear colleague before bidding him farewell for the last time. With some sadness he read the words of Robert Clarke. "They didn't come home." As he loosened his grip and looked up toward Brace, he felt something hit his shoe. He glanced down while passing the papers across his desk to her. On the rough grey carpet to the left of his shoe was what appeared to be a small key.

Brace noticed his attention was elsewhere. 'Have you dropped something, Jason?'

'No, ma'am, that's everything. I'll just put my "away from office" message on and that's me done, so to speak.'

'Okay, that's good. Take care, Jason.'

'Thank you, ma'am. See you in a few weeks.' Hingston leant toward his computer and Brace walked in the direction of her office. Intrigued and perplexed, Hingston scooped the object from the floor, into the palm of his hand. He opened his palm. There lay a dull brass key, about an inch and a half in length, minimalistic in design with an oval shaped bow. There were no markings on it and Hingston had no answer as to its origins or more interestingly, how it had apparently slipped from his paperwork to come into his possession.

'Rob?' he called across the office. 'Have you put anything on my desk?'

'No, sarge.' He began to give a broad grin. 'Would I be so careless? I'd never see it again!'

Hingston shook his head. He looked at the key again. There was something about its simplicity that he liked; its cool, smooth, metallic presence. He noted it appeared particularly old, possibly antique. A ream of questions sped through his head. How did it find itself within his paperwork? Why was it there? What is its significance, if any? Feeling unexpectedly content, he slipped it into his jacket pocket and got back to shutting down his computer.

* * *

The traffic between Chiswick Police Station and Hatch End was clear and Hingston closed the burgundy gloss painted door to his 1930s semi at the exact moment the grandfather clock chimed one.

He dropped himself into the sofa and touched his jacket pocket. The cool metal of the key felt pleasant against his fingers as he placed it down on the glass coffee table. For several minutes Hingston sat in silence staring at it and his mind rapidly processed and rejected reams of hypotheses for its appearance in the Clarke investigation file.

He felt let down by the system. Signed off; out of harm's way as far as the investigation team and the force were concerned, next appointment in three weeks and between now and then, isolation, with no direction other than to rest and relax.

He got up to prepare a sandwich and thought back to his Occupational Health assessment. Brace was correct, he had not been sleeping. What she didn't know was why. Shortly after the Clarke twins' disappearance, Hingston began to experience a series of night terrors or Pavor Nocturnus as Occupational Health advised. In under an hour from falling asleep the innocent opening scenes would play out. Every night it was the same:

Muted rays of light illuminated a vast, summer meadow. The meadow glowed with warmth. It was saturated with life. There was no place for imagination.

Tall grasses and fluffy seed heads nodded. A distant songbird beautified the scene with its music, amplified from oak trees that towered over fields that rolled into the golden horizon.

The air was silky and perfumed by heady honeysuckle that hypnotised. It carried the sound of rapid footfalls and trouser legs pushing through grasses. A curly haired boy ran tirelessly into the meadow. His white shirt billowed between his braces, his slender body was silhouetted beneath its drapes and his blond hair bounced with each stride.

The pace was set; the energy infectious; the freedom inspiring. The promise of adventure increased with every breath. Thus the dream grasped Hingston so tightly that it was impossible for the boy to continue to run alone.

Only when the boy splashed through the clear, shimmering brook, did the sickening ache of death seep into Hingston's bones.

The boy ran on, cloaked by a December night and his laboured breath condensed, emitting swathes of tiny silver stars that mirrored those above. The damp grasses chilled and his knees ached, yet he refused to falter. Claret blood oozed and dripped. It clung like a suffocating mask and choked and stifled and tortured.

It mattered not how many times they began at the meadow. Hingston always ran with the boy. The agonising fear clung long after he awoke. But the memory of the brook and everything thereafter was always lost.

Hingston had never previously experienced night terrors and was left shaken and tormented alone in his house every night. After twenty minutes the panic would subside, he would lay back down and attempt to go to sleep. In doing so, he would hear the familiar melodic chimes.

Occupational Health concluded the music was an hallucination and Hingston had no alternative explanation. Anxiety and insufficient rest were deemed the root cause of his problem and that was why he had been signed off for four weeks' recuperation.

As he sat back down with his lunch, he felt at a loss. Ordinarily, he would only take a few days off work at a time and that would be solely to work on the garden or the house and maybe the occasional visit to his parents or his uncle. It dawned on him that most of his childhood hobbies had been forgotten, for all of his energy was devoted to policing; the one thing he couldn't touch for several weeks.

Hingston didn't even consider a visit to his parents. They would undoubtedly ask him about Remi, his ex-girlfriend of two years past, and that would only annoy him. He regretted they were no longer together, especially when the reason for the break up was, in retrospect, so insignificant. But he was now quite satisfied on his own – provided he has his policing.

* * *

Hingston spent much of the afternoon recounting the Clarke case, in an attempt to discipline his fears and convince himself that he *had* conducted a thorough investigation.

It was at 10.37 p.m. on Friday the 15th of April when a panicked Mrs Clarke telephoned the police control room and reported her twins missing. Despite the calm and reassuring tone of the experienced call handler, Mrs Clarke blurted and stumbled her way through her account before her husband came on the line and reiterated a coherent set of facts with a measure of parental opinion. Their twin boys had not come home from school. "They are good, well behaved teenagers who *always* come home from school and they *always* walk home with their younger brother, Robert, who is thirteen. The school confirmed at 4.20 p.m. that they were not on school grounds. It is *totally* out of character for them to fail to answer their mobile phones or to respond to text messages." Throughout the evening Mr and Mrs Clarke had phoned the parents of their boys' school friends and they remained unlocated. Mr Clarke went to the school grounds and to the local park to look for the boys and drew a blank. They had not expected them to be there, however, because they knew their boys would not be disobedient. It was now very late, so they called the police.

From the start, their disappearance did not meet the regular criteria for kidnap; the boys were five foot nine and presumably, both being missing, they left the school entrance together, thereby being able to put up a fight if one were required. There were no police reports of a struggle or unusual activity in the area. A CCTV search provided no evidence whatsoever. The Hi-Tech Crime team found nothing to steer the investigation one way or the other; their social networking activity had ceased, as had their mobile phone usage, and their cyber history revealed only what appeared to be two regular schoolboys who made no suggestion they planned to leave home.

The boys ran a daily paper round before school every morning and had done so for over three years. Their earnings were generally frittered away on sweets, magazines and computer games, according to their parents, who were convinced the boys would not have been flush with cash. They did not have bank cards.

The school confirmed that they were present for their geography lesson which was the last period of the day and considered that these average achievers led average lives and held no concerns for their academic or social skills; they were two of a large crowd of friends who they had shared since starting their GCSE course criteria in September. Their peers seemed to be either non-committal, generally vague, possibly totally unobservant or self-consumed. The most meaningful account was provided by a fourteen-year-old girl who said "I think I saw Nathan and Dan stood on the corner of Latymer Gardens, not really doing anything, just stood there talking to each other at about 3.55 p.m.". Latymer Gardens is in the opposite direction to Bishop's Avenue where their brother, Robert Clarke, was waiting for them. If this girl's recollection was accurate, then it appeared that the twins had no intention of meeting their brother by four p.m.

A statement had also been taken from the owner of the newsagents who considered them to be efficient, hard workers who were very quiet; in the years he had known them they kept themselves to themselves and politely got on with their rounds. He confirmed that they did not collect their week's pay after school on Friday the 15th of April. They usually stopped by between five and five thirty p.m. after they had returned home and changed out of their school uniform. Their salary totalled £25 which they shared for running two rounds back to back each weekday.

Hingston suspected the twins had executed a well organised plan to run away by purposefully leaving no social footprint which could be traced online or offline. Had they stopped at the newsagents to collect their pay they would have been caught on camera inside the shop. Had they gone home first they would have faced unavoidable conversation with Mum who stated to police she always asked about the fine detail of their comings and goings from the house. Had they confided in their school mates perhaps one may have buckled under the pressure by now, almost a month since their disappearance. Surely, if the boys had been tempted in a surge of hormonal defiance, to do something wildly out of character just to give it a go, be daring and test their parents' boundaries, they would have been home within twenty-four hours. There had to be an answer; a reason, a discovery and an outcome, but it remained buried by questions and painfully out of reach.

* * *

Hingston opted to get an early night. The night terrors and the tossing and turning were exhausting him. He chose the sofa to avoid the bedroom. Maybe a change of surroundings would help. The key would be right in front of him. It would give him something tangible to focus his mind away from the panic should it occur. He lay down, cradled by the cool leather and thought of the roses in the front garden in full bloom. Lustrous shades of crimson, fire opal and gold; soft pink and cream to offset and enhance their vibrancy; the sweet and mellow fragrances that uplift and refresh passersby; the burgundy front door framed perfectly by bulbous flower heads and rosebuds dappled with dew on an early morning. A fresh start was what Hingston needed and he drifted off to sleep as the leather warmed around him.

'Jasper!' Hingston hollered as he hurled himself off the sofa, hitting the coffee table in his stampede to the hallway. Gasping for breath he steadied himself in the doorway, shaking and dripping sweat from his brow and top lip. 'Jasp…' Each intake was insufficient and the hollow, hooting, horrendous sound on inhalation scared him more. Almost doubled over, he stumbled back towards the coffee table. The sweat had run in his eyes and made them stream; he fought for his breath and felt for the key. It had been knocked off the table and he fumbled manically in search of it. Coughing with saliva running down his chin, his fingertips detected the metal. With some relief he pulled himself up onto the sofa. Heart racing, he lay on his side and clenched the key in his fist, wiping his face with the sleeve of his shirt.

The delicate chimes began to play. He shuffled himself into a half seated position and began to relax his fist. Four deep fingernail marks and part of the oval bow had indented his palm. As he looked at it, hand trembling, the music became louder.

'Jasper?' Hingston recalled this name; the only verbal memory of any of his night terrors. Was the curly haired boy Jasper? Was he really chasing this boy? Had he seen the boy's face, but was unable to remember? Before he knew it, he was off again; more questions, same subject, *no* answers.

Determined to conquer this unwanted condition, he walked to the kitchen and poured a glass of water from a bottle stored in the fridge. He had caught sight of the wine stood next to it, but thought better of it. He needed to relax. That, he discovered this first afternoon, was going to be difficult for him. He must get away!

Chapter Two

Reflections on a Postcard

The grandfather clock chimed ten. Two hours ago, Hingston had been trying to get to sleep, but now he was wide awake. He picked up his phone and searched for his uncle, Zachary Hingston.

Zachary or Uncle Zack "The Whack" was in his sixties, a keen sportsman and since retirement, a degree calibre history buff. He excelled at cricket and in his day would notch up sixes on the pitches in and around Dartmouth on a routine basis. Uncle Zack never seemed to change his appearance; a colourful polo shirt with the discreet embroidery of either a golfing or a sailing brand; Levi's jeans, for he always tried to be trendy; muscular, tanned arms from his sporting and gardening activities; short cut hair which had turned grey when he was thirty; kind blue eyes, deep crow's feet from plenty of laughing, a prominent Roman nose and a broad smile.

'Jason! What a lovely surprise! How are you, my boy?' Uncle Zack's tone was warm and sincere. 'Now, I hope you've rung me with a date you're planning to visit?' He always asked more than one question at a time which would serve him poorly if he were a detective.

Hingston used this to his advantage, ignoring the first question and responding with, 'How does tomorrow sound?'

'Tomorrow? Well... the place is a bit untidy 'cause I'm refitting the kitchen, but if you don't mind lending us a hand? Why not, son?'

Hingston immediately felt uplifted. As he ended the call he wondered if he had been unfair to Uncle Zack in failing to comment on how he was. He'd been deceitful, but he knew Zack would have wanted to get back to his televised sport.

* * *

At four a.m. Hingston was on the road. Just past Stonehenge his mobile rang. It was Uncle Zack.

'It's your Aunt Beryl,' said Zack. 'She's broken her leg and I'll be staying with her for a while in Truro.'

'Oh dear. Not too badly I hope,' Hingston replied. Aunt Beryl was Uncle Zack's eldest sister.

'Just the one, clean break. If you still want to come, you can, but you'll be on your own and the place's a tip. You'd have to live on takeaways. It's up to you.'

'Yeah, I can manage with that. What I live on at work! Besides, that kitchen of yours needs doing. Perhaps I can make myself useful and show you I didn't take after Dad!'

'Ha! Look, Jason, make yourself at home and don't feel obliged to get things moving on the kitchen. I'll leave the key under the doormat.'

'For goodness sake!'

'What?' said Zack.

'Do the Hingstons never read the papers or keep up with the times?'

'Ah, this is policeman plod speaking I see.'

'Basic security and sensible precautions.'

'Jason, this is Dartmouth we're talking about. Don't get crime down here!'

Hingston knew there was no reasoning with him and so simply wished his aunt well.

'Okay, my boy. I recommend the chippie off Lower Street.'

* * *

Hingston took an early evening walk along Dartmouth's cobbled quayside to the historic Bayard's Cove Fort. Its solid and rugged presence seemed to protect the colourful townhouses in the same way a marble bookend supports a collection of paperbacks. Hingston felt equally protected as he stepped through the wide, irregularly shaped archway into the fort and found himself a place to sit in one of the gunports facing towards the sea. It was here, with his legs dangling above the River Dart, that he felt comfortably alone and with the expanse of the river stretching out into the sea he felt free.

A cool sigh of sea air brushed across Hingston's eyes and made him blink. It seemed a little darker than he remembered. He tried to blot out the sound of the seagull and catch hold of his previous thoughts which had felt so significant. His attempt to remember was in vain and he knew it. He therefore wondered just how long he had been daydreaming.

The Indian restaurant beckoned. Hingston thought about the surge of tangy fragrances which danced exotically each night through Dartmouth's historic streets; a combination which brought to mind the sixteenth century sailors and their perilous journeys to worlds which were once merely imagined by most and where the treasures brought back were tasted by few.

'No wonder Dartmouth is haunted,' Hingston mused. He levered himself up and, in a crouched position, turned around. To his surprise, he found himself facing a pair of legs. And a stick.

'Good gracious!' said the woman as she peered down at him.

Hingston lost his balance and almost toppled backwards. Concerning him most was the thought of rolling out of the gunport. 'Sorry,' he apologised and got to his feet, slightly shaken and unimpressed by the presence of the elderly woman. 'I had no idea you were there. I didn't hear you approach and I had been sat here for, well, a good time.'

'Yes, I had been watching you.'

Her admission surprised Hingston. He looked at the woman's grey hair, pulled softly into a low bun. Her rather drab and undistinguishing attire comprised of a white blouse, navy trousers and a long, baggy, navy cardigan. Her shoes were plain and partly obscured by the trousers and her stick had carvings along the handle of a floral nature. Her face was heavily lined and it was impossible to tell if she had spent many decades frowning or laughing or whether she was just incredibly old and had spent all her life on the coast being weathered like the fort.

Hingston focused on her green-grey eyes which were scanning him all over and he decided to interrupt her assessment of him. With his left arm outstretched aside the gunport wall, he moved towards the woman in an effort to gain a position of full height. 'Excuse me, madam.' Hingston gave a smile and raised his eyebrows, again gesturing with his arm to indicate his desired direction of travel.

She looked into his eyes. Hingston noticed a small scar across her left eyebrow. Her eyes, now still, gleamed calmly from their position behind folds of skin. She stood there motionless, staring.

'May I move away from the gunport, please?' He was now starting to assess the situation a little more closely. 'Are you okay, madam?'

'Oh, yes.' With that she stepped back and Hingston moved into the fort.

The fading light flashed on the river and Hingston decided to leave. As he began to turn away, his attention was drawn to a rapid slapping of footsteps. They were coming into the fort. A boy ran past him. It was only a fleeting glimpse Hingston caught as the boy disappeared through a passageway towards stone steps which led around the outside of the fort. The boy appeared to be about nine-years-old and Hingston wondered why he was out, alone and running around.

'Jasper!' The name was shouted with great force and its familiarity turned Hingston's head in the direction of its source. There was a dark haired woman, kitted out in tight jeans and a low cut, stripy top, yellow gold bangles jangling on her right wrist as she swung her arms and marched purposefully in the direction of the boy; her ankles slightly wavering as she drove her stiletto sandals over the craggy paving. 'Jasper!' She looked at Hingston in what could only be described as fury. 'Have you seen that little sod?' she barked.

Hingston gestured towards the stone steps. This woman was not local. Her accent and her appearance suggested to Hingston she would have been better placed behind the bar of an East-end club. She rolled her eyes and batted her false lashes in impatience as Hingston stepped aside, giving her space to storm past.

'Get down here now!' she pointed downwards with her inch-long, crystal embellished nail and glared up the steps.

'You never let me have any fun,' the boy whined. 'Why couldn't we have gone on an exciting holiday?'

She ignored his question and continued to point with such determination it looked like she was trying to shoot a lightning bolt from her finger. 'There's a man stood here and I don't want you making a scene.' She began to drop her gaze and Hingston could tell the boy was now following her orders, walking down the steps.

As he reluctantly slouched past her with his head flopped to the side and with a hint of juvenile defiance, she continued to fix her eyes on him as if his head were a ball of alnico and her eyes discs of iron.

'Move,' she demanded.

'Take a chill pill,' the boy retorted.

'Don't you get mouthy with me! Where did you get that expression from?'

The boy pursed his lips together. She bent her knees and looked him in the face.

Hingston had by now repositioned himself further down the fort, looking out at the river. The name Jasper felt so significant it could have been scribed on every boat and reflected on every crest of water. He kept a covert eye on the domestic which was reaching its climax.

'Jasper. I *said* where did you get that from? I think you're in enough trouble as it is, don't you?'

No reply came.

'One, two…'

'Dad,' the boy mumbled.

'Your father!' the woman screeched.

Hingston thought the father may have made a valid comment, but his flippancy had now got his son and himself into trouble.

'Right. You're coming back into that restaurant and apologising for throwing a tantrum. Your father will pay the bill and then *he'll* have some explaining to do.' With that, she grasped the boy's hand and marched him out of the fort with the same gusto with which she had entered.

Almost instantly, the fort fell silent and the air was fresh. Hingston's attention returned to the old woman who was watching *him* and showing no interest in the events involving Jasper and his mother.

Before he could comment, the woman said, 'Keep an open mind and allow your thoughts to ebb and flow like the sea. That is the key to solving your problem.' Her eyes remained fixed on his and she began to laugh. Not in a mocking way, but in the manner of a wise school teacher who shares a nugget of information with a child and watches it slowly register.

Hingston recognised this laugh, but wasn't convinced he'd entirely grasped the point of her comment because he was busy trying to work out how she knew he had a problem and moreover, how she had drawn this conclusion from simply looking at him. He then began to wonder why she had taken such an interest.

'You must be a local.' Hingston seized the opportunity to gain control of this exchange and visualised the comfortable and familiar cosiness of an interview room.

'I am a regular visitor of Bayard's Cove, yes.'

Hingston recognised the ease at which the woman tiptoed around his question to provide an almost acceptable response whilst failing to answer it. 'Do you live in Dartmouth?'

'I knew *you* didn't, the way you walked in here,' she stated coldly.

Hingston cast his mind back to the cobbled street; the irregularly shaped archway; the fort with the eleven empty gunports; he recalled the family eating fish and chips who he passed when walking along the cobbles and the quiet solitude when he reached the fort. The absence of any elderly woman from his memory made him uneasy.

She gave him a small smile, which did nothing to reduce his suspicion or stop his frantic processing. Hingston observed her reddened hands resting motionless at her sides; her right, holding her walking stick; her left, absent of any jewellery. Perhaps he had simply forgotten her, for he was very tired, or perhaps she was camouflaged by her dreariness or maybe she lived in one of the "paperback" townhouses.

The woman opened her mouth as if to speak, then stopped, appearing to take a moment's thought. 'Would it make you more comfortable if I told you the fourth house down from the fort is mine?'

Hingston was taken aback by her question; unprecedentedly flummoxed by her command of the conversation and her apparent ability to second-guess him, or worse, read his mind. His immediate consideration was yes, if it is true. Instead, he replied, 'That's very nice. Not many people have the luxury of such beautiful views.' He gave her a nod. 'Have a pleasant evening,' he said.

'You didn't answer my question,' the woman stressed with a sudden air of impatience.

Hingston felt a pang of annoyance, bearing in mind she had cleverly avoided all of his. Where could she have been standing when he walked into the fort? The fourth house would only have afforded her a line of sight if she was stood on the doorstep or hanging out of a window. He thought of all the "no comment" interviews endured over the years, either as a result of the tactics of a legal advisor or the sheer bloody-mindedness of an obnoxious detainee.

'I've got to go now. Running late for dinner.' Hingston didn't try to soften his tone or make his excuse appear more plausible by checking his watch. He began to walk away in the direction of the town.

'Hiding from your fears is certainly not the key to solving your problem,' she called after him and her words resonated like a perfectly struck tuning fork.

Hingston paused and then continued to walk away. Frustrated with himself as much as with the old woman, he brooded on her last words. Her interference was not wanted.

A refreshing waft of air blew in from the river and a passing seagull sounded a melancholy call as it swooped over the fort.

'So *this* is your house, is it?' Hingston muttered as he reached the fourth house from the fort. It was painted pale lemon, a bowl of fruit stood upon a lace doily in the window and a name plaque was fixed to the right of the front door which read "The Lookout". For some reason Hingston smiled when he read these words. He urged himself to *get a grip*; too little sleep, too much stress and too much driving must have made him overreact. He now felt desperate to resolve what he considered to be crazy, immature fears about the old woman being psychic or worse, another hallucination. He gave himself a moment to reassess the situation.

He reasoned that it may simply be her years of people-watching that made her uncannily intuitive and thought his curtness may have been unjustified. Furthermore, should he return to the fort, he realised it was likely he would bump into this "regular visitor" again. He decided he should have left on a pleasant note. With that, he turned around, placed his hands in the pockets of his lightweight pea coat and strode towards the fort.

The woman was not in sight as he approached, nor as he entered under the archway. Despite his best efforts to remain calm and measured, Hingston found himself regressing into a state of anxiety. Perhaps her absence was an attempt to unsettle him? Maybe he wasn't going to be able to find her because she was never really there? He walked across the centre of the fort, scanning the gunports in turn. As he neared the far side, he heard her voice singing an unrecognised ditty, the words of which he could not make out.

'Madam?' he called as he stepped through the passageway into a small, paved standing area which had a direct view out to sea. She was not there. The only sound was the water lapping against the rocks and being sucked back.

He rested his hand on the metal balustrade and looked out across the river. As he peered over the balustrade he felt a pang of stupidity, for why would the old woman have ended up in the river and furthermore, she would have had to have taken her stick with her, for it was also nowhere to be seen. He did his best to ease off the smiling and suddenly thought she may be stood behind him. He turned around and somehow her absence surprised him more than her presence would have. He stepped back into the fort and was unquestionably alone.

* * *

Uncle Zack's kitchen *was* a tip. So was the living room which had morphed into a cardboard utopia fit for a tramp. Hingston had already cleared a seat on the sofa when he arrived in the morning. The daylight had revealed toast crumbs which had somehow found their way to the sofa underneath the boxes, carrier bags and yesterday's paper which crowded the seats like unwanted visitors.

His next task was to find a fork for his takeaway. Hingston was search trained and had conducted countless over the years, but rummaging through Uncle Zack's dishevelled and unlabelled boxes would be a challenge for the most systematic of officers. The boxes were deep and the content had already been upended by Uncle Zack. After five minutes, Hingston had located two knives and one spoon. He had considered eating at the restaurant, but in the absence of any company had decided to buddy-up with the television. He sighed and reached for the spoon.

Hingston did not share Uncle Zack's enthusiasm for sport. The remaining channels offered a poor selection of entertainment; a cheesy, American, romantic comedy; a reality show addressing health problems; a documentary about whales; yet another reality show with squabbling teenagers; the news and a history programme focusing on an archaeological dig. The dig seemed the most inspiring, so Hingston followed along but was only paying as much attention to the hairy, T-shirted, dusty archaeologist as he was to his curry and this did not total a lot because his thoughts were again on the old woman from the fort.

Specifically, Hingston mused upon her comment, which appeared to be part insightful, part riddle. If the key to solving his "problem" was to keep an open mind and let his thoughts ebb and flow like the sea, then the question remained, what "problem" was she referring to? The night terrors, the disappearance of the Clarke twins? Or both? Whilst he insisted to Brace and Occupational Health that the Clarke twins' case had not caused his current condition, he had to accept that this had all come about after their disappearance.

Hingston groaned. He did not want the peculiar old woman to trigger more questions for him to ponder. To his annoyance, she had left him with a pang of suspicion due to her elusive behaviour. He felt short changed in a childlike way by her expertly executed evasive answers and her searching comments made him feel uncharacteristically vulnerable. With that, he flicked onto the romantic comedy and focused on the floppy-haired, blue eyed, tanned actor with a wide, bleached grin who gave a manly laugh and then got slapped.

Chapter Three

A Summons

The red pillowcase was uncomfortably bright. Hingston had been woken by the sensation he was being cooked in a soufflé. He had left a six inch gap in the curtains to allow a glow from the street lights to enter Uncle Zack's spare bedroom, but this had long since been replaced with the Maytime sunshine which was beating on his head. With a quiet groan, Hingston turned over and patted down the pillow to try to read the bedside clock.

'Thirty-seven,' he yawned. He could only see the last two digits, so summoned the strength to lift his head and lean forward. 'Eleven!' He was shaken from his restful state and looked at the clock again. His eyes diverted to the other items on the bedside cabinet; a glass of water which had warmed overnight to allow bubbles of oxygen and nitrogen to heavily pattern the microscopic imperfections in the glass; a cubic tissue box; his mobile phone and the key which he had placed nearest the bed. Hingston stared at the key, realising that he had not touched it and nor had he moved for twelve hours; his first good night's sleep for almost a month. It dawned on him that yesterday was Friday the thirteenth and having always dismissed superstitions, he declared 'Not unlucky for me' and pulled back the curtains with a freeness of spirit rarely experienced after youth.

Hingston hurried to Dartmouth Harbour. Having sailed up the River Dart before, a cruise to Totnes was beckoning him to hop aboard and enjoy the skipper's quips; gaze at the undulating hills, decorated with dense woodland and segmented fields; admire the tiny villages nestled like kittens on a huge patchwork quilt; spot seals and seabirds and pass the boathouse at Greenway which inspired a fictional murder scene penned by his hero, Agatha Christie.

To his disappointment, the cruise had departed at eleven and the next was at three fifteen. However, his enthusiasm was still in credit. He decided instead to drive to Totnes, amble around the historic market town and return after an early fish and chip supper.

* * *

The dominant East Gate Arch loomed ahead of Hingston as he walked up Totnes Fore Street. He observed its clock face, bell tower and ornate weather vane and peered up at its thrupenny bit window, wondering what lay inside and how often, if at all, anyone peered back out. The arch spanned and adjoined the buildings once owned by merchants of the sixteenth and seventeenth centuries and which were now occupied by an eclectic mix of shops. On passing under the arch, Hingston continued up the hill, browsing the High Street windows and dodging the Saturday shoppers who included a surprising number of hippies, many of whom had continued to live their chilled, Bohemian lifestyle since the 1960s.

A display of Eastern charms, chunks of quartz, brass Buddhas and dream catchers overcrowded one window. Hingston noticed fairy lights twinkling from somewhere inside this tiny, dingy shop. A tuneless wind chime clanged as someone exited onto the sunny pavement and a strong waft of incense escaped with them. It was so pungent Hingston wondered whether it was required to cover the sweet perfume of cannabis, a fragrance familiar to him from occasions where sack loads of the psychoactive plants were temporarily held in police station corridors following raids of cannabis factories. As he passed the shop door, a collage of amateur adverts almost completely obscured his view inside, allowing a pink flyer decorated with blue stars to catch his attention. It simply read "Is there life after death?" and provided a scribbled mobile number. He stepped up to an empty area of glass and spied a drowsy shopkeeper with a cat on her lap, asleep.

'Is there life after death?' he muttered. 'Hard to tell.'

Five doors up was a militaria shop. To Hingston, this was a treasure trove; a dressing-up box which would have embellished his childhood days of trench warfare in the lounge; a time warp waiting to be explored and he eagerly stepped inside. Hingston's passion for militaria was ignited. He thought there could be some interesting information to share with his fellow members of the Met Police History Society. The collection of World War Two rifles, sub-machine guns, bren guns, bayonets and grenades filled an entire wall and the shelves upon which some of them stood were decorated with shells and bullets lined up like tin soldiers in size order.

A small collection of mannequins were dressed in officers' tunics in khaki, field grey and postbox red and on the tunics were flourishes of medals. Propaganda posters provided a poignant backdrop and Hingston imagined the punchy, influential messages outpouring from the mouths of the leaders who once occupied the uniforms and the dire outpouring of blood as a consequence. Suddenly, the final words of Robert Clarke's statement rang in his ears with a renewed sadness. "They didn't come home." As Hingston reflected, the shopkeeper stepped in to seize the opportunity to bring the objects back to life with such a deep, booming voice it was as if a No. 5 Mills bomb had exploded.

'Splendid example of a German veteran's tunic; one of the best. The insignia and awards are all original. You'll see das Deutsche Kreuz in Gold, the German Cross in Gold, embroidered on the right pocket, here, which marks an outstanding achievement and opposite, on the left pocket, das Eisernes Kreuz Erste Klasse, the Iron Cross First Class, which the brave chap would have won prior to the Cross in Gold. The Iron Cross, as I'm sure you'll know, is the most famous German war decoration.'

Hingston replied to the tall, sturdily built enthusiast with a solemn nod.

'And this superb Royal Artillery uniform complete with three rank pips indicating the rank of Captain is a wonderful addition to any collection.'

Hingston pointed at the medal ribbons. 'Yes, there's his Military Cross… Pip, Squeak and Wilfred and… the 1939-45 Star.'

The shopkeeper smiled and Hingston saw a flash of a gold premolar. 'So are you a collector?'

'Not especially,' said Hingston. 'I read, tune into the history channels.'

'Then I suggest you take a look at the selection of books in the corner.'

'Ah. Now that's different,' Hingston remarked on lifting up a paperback, 'World War One and Two. A Touch of the Supernatural.'

'It's a good read. Highly recommend it. I also keep a copy in the window; it attracts a lot of chaps and chapesses you wouldn't normally see in a militaria shop.'

'Those that frequent the shops displaying ads about life after death I suppose?' Hingston laughed.

'Don't mock it,' said the shopkeeper. 'There's many folk down this part of the country who believe in the supernatural. I'm talking about Wicca and witchcraft; blessings and ill-wishes; pixies, fairies, wood nymphs and ghosts.' He raised his eyebrows higher. 'I may think it's historic mumbo jumbo, but it sells books and I'm not going to miss out on sales.' The gold premolar was shining again. He approached the display and plucked out a copy.

Hingston realised the shopkeeper had rehearsed both his patter and his showy presentation when he flicked open the book and without looking at the page, began to pontificate about the photograph of a World War One squadron. Hingston knew that if his grandfather had been standing with him, he would have muttered a disparaging remark or two. "Swankpot" came to mind. As Hingston reminisced, his attention was drawn to the shopkeeper's index finger which was now jabbing at the photograph like a frenzied woodpecker.

For someone who professed disbelief in "mumbo jumbo" the shopkeeper conveyed convincingly his confidence in both the integrity of the photograph and whatever paranormal association came with it. Hingston decided to listen.

'...the ghostly apparition, clear as day, bold as brass,' said the shopkeeper. 'Recognised by all of his squadron. Dead two days, yet present with his comrades and taken on the day of his funeral.' The shopkeeper noticed Hingston's general expression of scepticism and shut the book, gave a cunning wink and announced, 'You've got a timeless face. Classical looks. I'll do you a deal on any of those tunics; twenty percent off, today only!'

A short while later and absent of any purchases, Hingston continued his way up the narrow High Street. The Saturday afternoon browsers began to diminish and the shops were replaced by restaurants, estate agents and the odd privately owned property.

Suddenly, a bristly mongrel came into view, scampering down the hill towards Hingston. Its paws scratched along the pavement like someone playing wire brushes and its tongue flapped from the side of its mouth. Its head was cocked and Hingston thought it may have been coming over to be petted. Instead, the dog gave a soft yap, took a ninety degree turn, darted across the road and disappeared down a side alley he hadn't noticed. Hingston's enquiring mind forced him to investigate.

The alley was narrow. Upon closer inspection there was a small plaque fixed to the brickwork. Above a roughly painted arrow were the words "Bric-a-Brac". An orange-brown hue stained the plaque in two vertical streaks which had leached from rusted screws.

In the direction of the arrow at the end of the alley was a shabby building of two storeys which had three very dirty windows and a door, ajar. Hingston assumed the dog had scooted through the gap and that the shop was probably owned by an equally scruffy man.

On stepping over the threshold, a strong, musty aroma made Hingston's nose tingle. There was a competing smell which wafted from a hair-ridden dog basket and a buzzing noise with a prominent beat which suddenly stopped.

'Hi ya.' A gloomy looking teenager wearing headphones was stood behind the counter, propping himself up against a bookcase filled with all manner of items, but not a single book.

The moment Hingston replied with, 'Afternoon, just browsing,' the teenager tapped the MP3 player held in his hand and blotted him out.

The shop clearly used to be a house. There were several small rooms set off a single corridor upstairs and down. On each step of the narrow, windy staircase was an example of bric-a-brac or in Hingston's opinion, junk, including old telephones, vases and dolls. As Hingston walked through the rooms they reminded him of Uncle Zack's upended boxes. Collections of kettles sat next to smoked mirrors with elegant and not so elegant images of women painted upon them, one of which even took Hingston a moment to fathom out. Partly complete crockery sets and dining room chairs were clumped together amongst hats, coat stands, board games with torn lids, a Space Hopper and a lab skeleton. Hingston stepped between the items littered across the room to examine a group of Wade china animals, only to discover each was chipped.

On picking his way back across the room, a cane toppled over into his path from where it had been resting against an umbrella stand. Hingston rolled his eyes and picked up the cane, placing it into the stand. His attention was drawn to an item sat just behind on the floor. He crouched down and touched the dust which obscured the grain of this wooden, oblong box. Its overall appearance was plain. In fact, it was its demure anonymity amongst the surrounding chaos that spurred Hingston to pick it up.

The box was a foot long and it was obvious there was something inside due to its weight. To Hingston's frustration the lid was immovable. A keyhole was positioned on the front side of the box and Hingston returned its dark glare, undeterred. He tilted the box away from himself, hoping to see a key taped to the base. He sighed and checked for the same on the back. As he inhaled, his breath caught in his throat. He spluttered, blinked and as he refocused on the box, the honey coloured grain became hazy and he feared he may pass out.

He dropped to his knees, maintaining a firm hold on the box, unable to do little else but put his head forward and close his eyes. The spinning motion behind his forehead became a smooth rocking sensation and he slowly reopened his eyes. To his disbelief, the dim lit meadow was before him. It made him feel sick. He stared helplessly into the expanse and the scene became sunnier and brighter as if captured by time-lapse photography and played in reverse. When he noticed the absence of the curly haired boy, the brightness of the meadow increased tenfold to become a solid, brilliant gold before fading to a mellow honey colour and then the grain of the box reappeared. Instantly, the box became as clear and sharp as it was seconds earlier and Hingston felt fully grounded as if the episode had not occurred. However, he had been caught unexpectedly by the hallucination or mirage or whatever madness it was. He held the box to his ribcage. He got to his feet, made his way to one of the chairs and placed the box on it. He reached to his back pocket and pulled out his wallet. He flicked open his wallet with one hand as if he were about to show his warrant card and make an arrest.

He stared at his wallet, visualising the key on the bedside cabinet. In his rush to get to Totnes he had forgotten to take it with him. He looked at the ceiling. His eye sockets and cheeks were florid and throbbing with discomfort as if he had been burnt by the light of the golden meadow. He grimaced as he failed to contain two tears. A crescendo of emotion pulsated through his pulmonary system with a clash of frustration, desire and loss. He squeezed his wallet closed and thought of the officers in their khaki tunics with their stiff upper lips.

Having picked up the box, Hingston made his descent past the dolls, vases and telephones and stepped up to the counter. The wiry mongrel was sat in its basket inches from his feet and was panting through a smile in time with the buzz from the teenager's headphones. Hingston placed the box on the counter. The teenager was now engrossed in a magazine.

'Excuse me,' Hingston called.

Granted, the buzzing was louder than before, but the teenager's lack of awareness was so poor Hingston could have walked away with the box unnoticed.

'Excuse me,' Hingston called again and reached towards the boy, strumming his fingers on the page of the magazine.

The teenager jumped. 'Wo!' he said. He turned off his music, unpopped his headphones and his half-lidded gaze returned.

'I'm sure your boss would not be happy if items were nicked from his shop whilst you're in charge?' said Hingston.

The boy's eyes finally started to show a glimmer of realisation and after a moment's contemplation he replied, 'Don't get crime in Totnes.'

Hingston almost laughed. This familiar reply made him wonder whether all Devonshire residents shared this misconception. 'You need to keep your wits about you even if it's just for the purpose of customer service.' Hingston was not prepared to allow the teenager to have the last word. 'Now, I'm interested in this box that I found upstairs. It's locked. Do you have a key for it?'

The boy placed his hands on the ends of the box and tilted it away from himself.

'No, there's no key taped to the box,' Hingston interjected, but was pleased the boy showed some logic similar to his own.

'Dunno then,' the boy concluded and gave a yawn.

'How much is the box?' asked Hingston.

The boy again began to tilt the box.

'There's no price on it either,' Hingston added.

'Dunno then.' The boy scratched his cheek. 'I can ring my boss if you want?'

Hingston nodded. 'Thanks.'

The teenager turned to the bookcase behind him and reached for a pale biscuit coloured phone, mottled with ground-in grey marks. He dialled a combination of the four less grubby keys. 'Hi ya.'

Hingston smiled at the boy to acknowledge a call had been successfully made.

'Yeah. I've got a customer with a wood box he found upstairs. Yeah, it's wood. Yeah... yeah. Dunno.' He raised his head in an upwards nod at Hingston. 'Was it in the room with the lab skeleton?'

'Yes.'

'Yes,' relayed the teenager. 'He wants the price and the key. Sure… yeah… cool.' The receiver was clumsily replaced. 'Had the box for donkey's years. Always been locked as far as she can remember and never had a key. Thinks it came with the lab skeleton. To be honest, she's not sure what's in it or if it'll break when you try to get it open. So, forty quid, she said.'

'Forty quid!'

'Yeah. Never barters. Probably doesn't contain pickled specimens or anything that might've gone off,' the boy teased.

Hingston knew he couldn't leave it behind, his experience on finding it felt too significant. He sighed as he reached for his wallet to prise out two crisp £20 notes. The credit card slot in which the key should have been cradled lay empty. Hingston let the notes slip from his fingers onto the counter.

'All on a hunch,' Hingston mumbled to himself, a reluctant gambler who knew the odds were against him.

Chapter Four
Guard Them Against Lilith

Hingston was once praised for his "poise and punctiliousness". Twenty-one years later, the articulate annotation of Hingston's Head Teacher was still quoted by his family. Hingston sometimes wondered whether the Head Teacher had intended to set a standard for him to always strive to live up to, a mark under which he should never fall. As he kicked off his shoes in Uncle Zack's hallway, he paused, considered repositioning them into a neat pair, glanced into the living room and made for the stairs. The soft, cool carpet pile parted underneath his socks and as he ascended, two stairs per stride, the wood beneath cracked and creaked like an old Dartmouth galleon. The faint, fresh fragrance of his midday shower lingered on the landing and the sun had long since passed, leaving a gentle serenity in the bedroom despite Uncle Zack's bold colour scheme.

He held the box at arm's-length, moderated his breathing and felt his eyelids twitch, causing his eyes to dance around the pattern of the grain in the rhythm of a wild polka. They came to a sudden halt upon the keyhole and Hingston sat down on the thick duvet. He traced the perimeter of the keyhole with the same awe and cautiousness that would be applied if peering over the edge of a chasm. Steadying the box on his lap, he stretched toward the bedside cabinet and slid the key across the glass protective surface. A quiet clinking sound was created as it came over the edge before being sandwiched between his fingers and thumb. The brass began to warm as he manipulated it and aligned it with the lock. A rush of emotion, a surge of fear, anticipation and excitement, was trapped inside him by the vacuum-like silence of the room. A feeling of airlessness surrounded him and his hand trembled as the key was guided towards the keyhole.

The key glided into the chamber, filling the darkness as swiftly as Hingston's irises were overtaken by his pupils. Cool air finally rushed over his dried tongue and his nostrils tensed. He turned the key to the right. It barely moved and his moist thumb and finger slipped. He wiped his hand on the duvet. With greater force he broke through the resistance of the old lock with a crack and a clunk.

Hingston paused, dumbfounded, and stared in amazement. He fought through a crazy overload of thoughts. He felt confused. It was as if the last few days had been placed in a blender and the pulse button had been hit at differing intervals and durations a dozen times. The tangible, logical, hard facts had been jumbled and spliced together with the doubts, questions, frustrations and the forgotten peculiarities that had seemed irrelevant and worthless previously. As a result, performing under a haze of blue stars were the forlorn parents of the Clarke twins, but inexplicably they were old and withered. Brace was reading out Robert Clarke's statement, wearing a postbox red tunic and she dropped and then stamped on his "Best Detective" mug. Hingston saw himself come rushing to centre stage and with a carved wooden stick he poked at the shards of the mug; golden light shone brightly from the pieces and he revealed the sparkling River Dart beneath. The river parted and a brass Buddha told him to "keep an open mind and let your thoughts ebb and flow like the sea" before it melted down and became the key. He shook his head as if he were trying to dislodge his thoughts, in the vain hope they would either reorder themselves in a logical sequence or exit his mind altogether.

His heart thumped as he loosened his trembling grip on the key and lifted the lid. The contents made it obvious that this was not the box from the old school science laboratories. The metal mechanisms looked magical and intricate; a lavish display of thousands of minute pins stood to attention around a long, chunky cylinder made from a golden tone of brass and a flat comb of regimented steel teeth lay alongside the cylinder, ready to be plucked. Hingston gazed in amazement, resting his hands on each end of the plain box.

The situation was almost incomprehensible. He recapped the events in reverse, questioning how this beautiful masterpiece could have ever found its way to the bric-a-brac shop, bashed about and unloved on the outside, locked with a key that had been lost at least decades before and most perplexingly, how that key had appeared at Chiswick Police Station in his paperwork. Hingston could not understand why this was happening to him. He had always huffed at any suggestion that fate existed and to have one of his core beliefs challenged, threw him into panic. Whilst he scrambled for an alternative answer, his mind began to play the chimes he knew so well. He felt his cheeks flush. Whereas the chimes had always soothed his anxieties, they now had the opposite effect. He felt as though the last remaining scraps of logic were being dragged from his grip into a powerful vortex. Clearly before him was a musical box, but what did it play and how did it operate? The music in his head stopped abruptly.

Hingston focused on a narrow, open compartment at the right of the box. It was created by a delicate wooden panel and was packed out with tightly folded, beige paper. He eased out the stubborn wad of paper, placed it on the duvet and looked into the compartment. There was another item. He lifted out an embroidered handkerchief and wrapped inside was a large steel key. It was a good three inches long with a substantial bow and was weighty. It appeared to have had its teeth sawn off leaving only the cylindrical shaft, however, there was a square shaped hole tunnelled up its length.

Hingston examined the box for its winding mechanism. Inside, to the left of the box, was a small scroll shaped hook which appeared to hold the end in place. He fumbled, but soon eased the hook open and the end of the box dropped down to reveal a slot for the key and three small, square shaped, metal buttons. Ignoring the throbbing in his ears, he inserted the key and with some difficulty wound it twice, creating two deep and hollow clackering sounds as the spring was tightened. No music played. Everything about the mechanism appeared so immaculate that Hingston was surprised but unperturbed by the silence.

He pressed the nearest button to no effect. He pressed the second which pivoted towards him and a dull, quiet thud sounded as the mechanism sprang into life. He was surrounded by the dynamic energy of the rich, bubbling melody that filled the room and which was *identical* to that he had come to rely on. With the speed of an anaesthetic, the beauty of the sound washed away his panic and drew him into a state of meditation.

Feeling serene, as if he were drugged, he placed the musical box onto the bedside cabinet as the last pins plucked the final notes. The room fell silent again. He collected up the winding key, handkerchief and wad of paper, swung his legs up onto the bed and dropped backwards with his head cushioned by the red pillow. There he lay, calmly deliberating, deducing and debating all manner of implausible explanations for this chain of events. The beige paper remained in his right hand. He brought it up close and as he stared, he could make out the grey text. It read "Teeth! Teeth!! Teeth!!! Incorruptible Artificial Teeth" and boasted about dentistry "without the slightest pain" and teeth made of vulcanite and of gold which would cost a maximum of £8 for a full set.

Bemused, he flipped the folded piece of newspaper over and read an advertisement for "Kallensee's Great Circus" that was to visit Exeter on Wednesday the 17th of October.

A brief line highlighted the names of the Proprietor, Acting Manager and Clown: Kallensee, Bibbings and Crim. Hingston was intrigued by these names and began to tease apart the newspaper. It opened out with the appearance of a deconstructed origami creation, consisted of a third of a sheet, which had been purposefully cut, and at its head in bold capitals were the words "RSDAY, OCTOBER 11, 1866".

'Eighteen sixty-six!' Hingston whispered. He was stunned by the possibility that he may have been the first to open the musical box in almost one hundred and fifty years. He felt sad that it may have remained mute for all or most of this period. A hint of panic began to stir inside him again. The music had lost its calming control.

He found himself skimming the newspaper notices for farmers' clubs, markets and church service cancellations, and adverts for bitter ale, hair dyes, paraffin oil and pharmaceutical balsam for a variety of ailments. The small print was crammed into its space, back and front, maximising the takings of the newspaper press and most probably the chances of the reader developing myopia.

It was on the reverse that Hingston noticed the title "THE EXETER AND W".

'Western Times? West Devon Chronicle?' Hingston suggested to himself.

He remembered the handkerchief and sat upright, picked it up and allowed it to flop open in his hands. There was more embroidery upon it than he had first noticed. The edge was decorated with tiny strawberries which formed a complete border. In the centre were the words "Train up a child in the way he should go and when he is old he will not depart from it". In tiny stitches beneath was the reference to Proverbs. To the bottom right Hingston read what he presumed to be the embroiderer's name Elizabeth Embling, and the year 1860. He then noticed in green stitches, close to the strawberry foliage and running in parallel to it, a series of names: Sarah, George, Charles, Louisa, John, Neville. He concentrated on the tiny, immaculate needlework and tried to imagine Elizabeth Embling sat in a grand house, stitching her handkerchief with love and devotion for her six children and the musical box adorning the drawing room with its magical aura of sound.

* * *

The paper bag with the large, smiling blue fish printed on it was of a generous size to accommodate the generous helping of thick cut chips and a huge piece of battered cod. Less than a minute from Uncle Zack's recommended chippie Hingston located a bench. The faint cheery voices of diners and social drinkers faded in and out as the evening sea breeze blew across the river and cooled his nose and ears. He tore the bag open, drove in the fork and shovelled three chunky flakes of meat into his mouth. His eyes began to water and he inhaled and exhaled, flicking the cod around his mouth with his burnt tongue.

He reached for the napkin and observed the steam billowing from the hole in the batter. He stabbed a chip with the two stumpy prongs of the fork and touched it on his parted lips.

'Bit of a perfectionist aren't you?'

Hingston jumped, knocking the chip onto the pavement.

Her green-grey eyes had lost their gleam and her features were blurred together in the low light of the evening. 'Oh, *I* startled *you* this time. Sorry,' she smiled.

This was not quite as Hingston remembered it. He peered at his chip lying on the pavement between his bench and that the old woman was sat on. With a loud flapping sound and a solitary ethereal caw, the chip was gone. Hingston watched the cleptoparasitic bird swoop across the water, bear to its left, rise and take a perfect gliding turn to boast about the golden chip that was protruding from its beak as if it were a Gurkha cigar. As he watched the gull continue its course back past his field of vision and down river, he was sure it gave a wink.

'As cocky as an opportunistic thief,' Hingston mumbled. He looked across at the woman who appeared to have been undistracted by the gull, her poise and expression unchanged, her eyes calmly on him. For three seconds he scanned her attire; the familiar bun, stick, navy and white simple clothes, waiting for her to comment on something. Anything. He turned to his cod and glanced back at her. No change. Fork prepared, he was about to select a second chip, but her presence had become overbearing. An uncomfortable consideration struck him. Perhaps she has died? A stream of possibilities surged as he looked across at her: an aneurysm; shocked by the gull; very old age and bad timing (for him)? Could he be hallucinating? He studied her static state, mildly concerned, oddly amused.

'Very quick to make judgements aren't you?' she sang softly from her seat.

Hingston felt his cheeks flush and his forehead tense into a frown.

'Over analysis is the brain's equivalent of sea fog. However expert the captain, his sense of direction is impaired. Frustration can become an interfering factor. There is a lot to be said for intuition and open-mindedness.'

The old woman's poetic psychoanalysis coupled with thoughts of his cooling cod prompted a reflex reaction only normally triggered by the interview of a divisive detainee. 'So you're telling me I'm a judgemental, narrow minded perfectionist who is frustrated by my problem?' The words stung his burnt tongue.

The old woman transferred some of her weight to her carved stick as she moved half a seat nearer to Hingston along her bench. 'I didn't directly connect your frustration with your problem such that your problem is the root of your frustration; rather that you have a tendency to become frustrated. Frustration is of course common in perfectionists when they have a problem; something you have now admitted you have.'

'Er, hang on. I haven't *admitted* anything and I don't understand why you are so keen to engage with me using these ridiculous riddles. To be frank, *you're* judgemental. Madam.' The fish and chips started to have less appeal.

'It is not always possible to *understand*,' she began to lean on her stick and rose from her seat. 'That is why you have labelled me as judgemental and...' She stopped and looked out to the river.

Hingston followed her line of sight and found nothing distinctive. From her standing position she was little more in height than Hingston was seated. He felt a mild pang of guilt as he did after exhibiting his terse behaviour at the fort yesterday. He rubbed his burnt tongue on the roof of his mouth and placed the heavy bundle of cod and chips on the bench beside him. The smiling fish was obscured. She began to walk away from Hingston in the direction of Bayard's Cove and the image of the pretty town house named "The Lookout" returned to his mind.

A few feet away she stopped and turned; not to look at him, but to project her voice and allow it to carry on the sea air. 'It was unnecessary to compare that gull to a criminal.'

Hingston suspected this was no more than a diversion on her part; the sentence she cut short surely had more meaning, however obscure, than her defence of a greedy sea bird. He tried to make amends. 'I wasn't comparing per se. After all, it was only a stolen chip and it's Devon. You don't get crime down here,' he smiled.

'No,' she scolded him and her eyes fixed on his. 'No. Foolishness and frivolity are friends of your foe and your foe will use them to get away with a felony.'

The seriousness of her tone connected Hingston with the woman as if he were sat at his desk discussing a case with his team. Taken aback by her forcefulness, he remained on the bench and watched in silence as the elderly woman turned and walked away. Again, she left her uncomfortable words reverberating in his head. As she stepped out of view his eyes drifted over to the water and he mused upon the saying "to have the wind taken out of your sails". Out of character, he left his dinner on the bench, but had a sense of satisfaction that a gull would soon swoop down and be happy.

* * *

He flicked off the light as the first few notes began to play. He climbed under the duvet and the hypnotic music entranced his senses and carried him to sleep like a lullaby. As the music slowed, Hingston's head began to move and his eyes twitched like the spikes on an electrocardiogram. His breathing rate increased and droplets of perspiration formed on his upper lip. After the last note was plucked and the steel comb lay rigid next to the still brass cylinder, Hingston turned back and forth, from one side to the other, gaining in pace as if he were attempting to transfer his energy to the musical box to make it play again. His breathing turned to panting and the panting to gasping. He grabbed and tussled with the duvet, pushing it and the space around him away. Whilst he won the fight with the duvet, throwing it from the bed, his internal panic continued. His legs kicked out as if he were running, he flung himself about and his face contorted between the breaths. With an agonising bellow he tensed his body, clenching his fingers and curling his toes, and with one sharp lunge he hit the floor. As his inner panic collided with the external shock he was forced out of his night terror. Like a child he cried. He reached across the carpet, pulled the duvet towards him and lay there shaking.

Half an hour passed before he unsteadily got to his knees, levered himself onto the bed and wound the musical box. As the chimes sang out he calmed and reached for the glass of water. He gulped it down to soothe his dry throat and mouth which had developed a bitter taste like that of sawdust and wood chippings. He felt a sharp pain in his head and wondered if he had hit it on the floor.

As he lay down and looked into the darkness of the bedroom, which was lit only by the glow of the street lights, his surroundings took on a rainbow of garish colours and he shut his eyes to escape the glare. There ran the boy through the meadow; the same pace, the same meadow, the same curls bouncing in the low summer evening light. He opened his eyes and the musical box was embellished with spangled shades of red, blue and silver. He shut them again, holding his head and the boy continued running. The rhythm of his stride fell in time with the melody and Hingston's breathing regulated to the same tempo. The boy ran through the shallow brook splashing his way up a bank and into another meadow where the sky turned royal blue, the meadow silver and the boy tripped and fell into a bed of metallic red strawberries. Instantaneously, the calm ended and Hingston gasped, flung himself upright and stared into the room. The rainbow of garish colours were before him again; like a kaleidoscope they broke into fragmented jewel shaped patterns and cascaded downwards from the ceiling into his lap, revealing his regular surroundings.

Hingston leant across and flicked on the light to the left of his bed. Laying in his lap was the handkerchief, the strawberries facing towards him, their bold colour shining in the artificial light. He read the children's names over and over like a mantra, circling the border before focusing on "Elizabeth Embling 1860". He ran his finger over the delicate stitches and felt a serenity pass into the room and embrace him lovingly. The notes of the musical box chimed the final two bars and as the silence engulfed him he felt peaceful and carefree.

He sat still, lost in the same dreamlike state as he had experienced at Bayard's Cove. In fact, it was the words of the elderly woman that very day which pulled him slowly back to the world of his bedroom with a smile.

'I'm keeping an open mind, Elizabeth Embling,' he said and switched off the light.

Chapter Five

Raindrops and Chocolate Ganache

'Thank you.' Hingston smiled as he welcomed a tall glass of hot chocolate and a slice of opera cake to his table.

The door to the cafe opened yet again and another group of holidaymakers bundled inside, bringing another series of watery footprints to the tiled floor. Their reddened cheeks had been buffeted and polished by the rain and wind. Within moments they scanned the occupied tables and met the stressed eyes of the waitress who hurried over, advised of the twenty minute wait and politely showed them back out of the door. The look of disappointment as they stepped onto the puddled cobblestones and their screwed up noses as they passed by Hingston's window seat, mumbling and gesturing at each other, made his hot chocolate seem all the more delicious. He took another sip whilst he waited for the cafe's Wi-Fi to connect with his phone.

The raindrops on the glass began to stream; the largest, heaviest droplets travelled down the surface, almost coming to a stop before colliding with stationary droplets to tip the critical mass and gain momentum again. Hingston considered the speed of the tumbling droplets to be similar to the cafe's Wi-Fi and he therefore made a start on the opera cake. He cut a large piece from the end of the slice and shovelled it into his mouth just as a second waitress, who had been idling away time at the till, walked past and asked if everything was all right with his order.

The chocolate ganache topping had adhered to the roof of his mouth and the creamy coffee and chocolate layers were oozing from the edges of the soft sponge. All he could do was nod and chew as he stared at the waitress who he hoped would hurry past.

She stood there with her head tilted to the side, gazing at him with her sixteen-year-old wide blue eyes, impatiently waiting for his chewing to stop.

He reached for his napkin and nodded some more as he brought it to his mouth to discretely confirm his order was 'very nice.'

'Is there anything else I can get you, sir?' she offered and gave a broad smile studded with braces.

'No, that's all, thank you.'

'Well, if there's anything else you want, just let me know.' She smiled some more, flicked her hair with her hand and gave a conspicuous wink.

A troop of colourful umbrellas bustled past the window which at this time of the year should have been colourful T-shirts and sundresses, or better still, the display of vibrant sails on the estuary at Salcombe, a short drive further west.

Hingston took another sip of hot chocolate and kept an impatient eye on his phone. *Finally* he had internet connection. He could now concentrate on the embroidered handkerchief which he hoped would unlock another layer of history and maybe provide clues to solve this bizarre series of events. Detective's logic made him select Neville first; last embroidered name, last child. He considered the biblical quotation on the handkerchief, on the balance of probabilities, was relevant to all six children, thus all would be under fourteen years at the time of embroidering. Date 1860; Neville no more than five years old, otherwise Sarah, the first child, may no longer be classed as a child. Within minutes he had a match. "Births Registered in October, November, December 1860: EMBLING, Neville Austin; Sub Registrars District, Crediton;

Volume 5b, page 99." He began to write details on the pale blue napkin whilst tucking into more of the opera cake. John, the second youngest, was registered in 1858; Louisa in 1856; Charles in 1853; George in 1853. Hingston paused with his biro implanted at the tail of the three and pressed the tip firmly into the napkin. He frowned.

'Charles eighteen fifty-three. George eighteen fifty-three,' he whispered. He looked back at his phone. Both were registered in Crediton and the volume and page numbers were identical. He decided to check again. There were two other George Emblings, but they were registered in Spalding and Oxford. There was only one Charles. Hingston acknowledged that the family may have relocated to the Crediton region. Maybe George was born in 1850 in Oxford and it was as simple as a move to the South West prior to the birth of Charles. 'Surely these boys were not twins,' he thought as a swathe of anxiety brought a chill to his chest.

'Sarah,' Hingston called impulsively, forgetting his surroundings. He began to prod at his phone to complete the search.

'Sophie,' a cheerful voice piped up.

Oblivious, Hingston stared at his phone, tapping his foot on the tiles as the page loaded.

'Sophie… it's Sophie. Not Sarah.' The blue eyes were upon him once again.

It was the name Sarah which shook him from his intense concentration. He looked up. 'Oh. Hello?'

'You called me,' she said, widened her eyes even more and pouted her lips.

Hingston stared back at her, unsure as to how this confusion had arisen.

'You called me,' she insisted, 'but it's Sophie. You called me Sarah by mistake.' The broad grin returned without delay.

He looked at her braces; alternate blue and pink caps. She was only young and Sarah Embling was his priority, so he decided to play it down. Ordinarily, he may have been tempted to banter and laugh it off. 'Oh!' he sang out with considerable inflection to stress without ambiguity that he now understood exactly what had happened. 'I'm sorry. I wasn't calling you over. I'm just doing an internet search and spoke my thoughts aloud. I'll keep quiet now and get on with my cake,' he nodded.

Her smile began to fade when it sunk in that her plan had failed.

Hingston felt quite relieved and his thoughts returned to Sarah Embling; the eldest sibling and where she had been born.

'You have nice brown eyes,' she giggled.

Hingston inhaled and pressed his teeth together.

'Excuse me, Sophie,' the stressed waitress interrupted and batted her eyes. 'I've just seated six at table three. Their order needs taking. Can you see to it, please?'

Sophie turned back to her colleague. She looked like she had just removed her face from a bucket of last week's fish. 'But I'm just seeing to this gentleman,' she complained.

The waitress glared and off Sophie went. 'Apologies, sir,' the waitress added. 'My little sister is a man-eater in the making and highly embarrassing.'

'That's okay. No offence caused.'

'In a few years she will have toned it down, believe me,' she said, gave a subtle wink and walked away, swinging her hips like the pendulum of his grandfather clock.

'Come on, Sarah,' he whispered as he scrolled down the page displayed on his phone. It was Crediton again. He caught his breath. Born 1849. There was no suitable alternative. George and Charles had to be twins. He felt it and somehow he knew it to be true. The children in this family were all registered in Crediton and they had twin boys amongst them. He felt cold inside but his face was hot with anticipation. The "whys" and "whats" flooded in and streamed together like the raindrops on the window. His head spun and his heart raced. Twin boys. *Twin boys.* What happened to the Emblings? Is there a connection between the Clarkes and the Emblings? If so, the appearance of the key *was* significant. There was a sudden halt.

The clinking of cups and cutlery; the continuous rumble of voices and peaks of laughter; the high pitched parps as the wooden chairs were readjusted on the terracotta tiles and the hustle and bustle of soggy customers in and out of the cafe were all lost to silence. Hingston could see the continuing activity, but could hear none of it. The fragrance of a fresh bake and the warming aroma of coffee had been snatched away with the mind bending speed of a magician's sleight of hand. An emptiness and detachment surged through his veins and shook him to the core. He tightened his grip on his biro and proceeded with another search on his phone, inputting a new criteria without blinking. The white background behind the black font burnt his retinas. It created a negative which flashed with every blink which followed when he forced his eyes away from the screen and onto the napkin. Repeatedly in his mind he read the words displayed on his phone. "EMBLING, Charles, 13, Crediton; Deaths December 1866."

The shrill screech of the kettle invaded his solitary cocoon and the life of the cafe returned with the ferocious boom of a fired cannon. It was at this moment Hingston felt strangely and wildly invigorated as if a race had just started and he was propelling himself forward with lightness and limitless energy, fuelled by freedom and excitement and anticipation. And then he felt the long grass tickling his hands. The dry taste of adrenaline overtook him and spurred him on faster through the meadow of his mind. He reached the shallow brook which splashed with each footfall but the water burnt like fire.

'Oh! Oh, oh, oh!' he heard.

'Wooah!' Hingston joined in Sophie's panic and stood up, shaking his hand which was stinging from a lashing of hot chocolate. The meadow felt like a distant memory and the pool of hot chocolate on his table began to drip over the edge and onto the floor.

'I'm *sooo* sorry. You'd been sat there so long I thought your hot chocolate must be cold, so I brought you a fresh one,' Sophie apologised. 'Let me mop this mess up.' Her blue eyes shone brightly against her flushed cheeks and she scanned Hingston rather than the mess she had created.

Hingston made a quick lunge toward his phone and rescued his napkin which was decorated with names and dates he did not want to lose.

'Here, let me sort you out,' Sophie fussed and plucked the napkin from his fingers.

'No…' Hingston interjected and teased the napkin back with a little more effort than he thought would be required and stuffed it into his pocket.

This prompted a reflex giggle as she gazed back at him.

The six old ladies on table three were clearly enjoying the furore and whispering about the skill deployed by Sophie to capture her prey.

He scratched his right eyebrow self-consciously.

The doe-eyed Sophie gazed at him for a few seconds before a large dishcloth was plonked into her hand by her sister, whose mood was now thunderous.

'*Table* then *floor*,' she ordered and pushed Sophie towards the table, maintaining a firm grip on Sophie's waist from behind.

Hingston produced a £10 note and placed it on the table. 'Don't worry about the change. Thank you.' Having managed to scoot through the small gap left by Sophie there was no more either of the waitresses could do to encourage him to stay or prevent his departure.

'Come by again soon,' Sophie called as he opened the cafe door. 'I'll make sure you get a free cake next time. Promise!'

As Hingston stepped onto the puddled cobbles he adjusted the collar of his pea coat to keep the rain out and made a dash to alternative shelter.

Around the corner and down the road he found a covered walkway and propped himself up against the window of a bakery. There, on his phone, was his last search showing the premature death of Charles Embling aged thirteen. To his surprise he still had a Wi-Fi connection. Hingston wiped the rain from his nose and cheeks and composed himself to search the records for Charles' twin, George. The dates of death and the ages did not correlate with the George Embling born in 1853. He sighed and stared out across the road and watched the rain.

Hingston heard a crescendo of wet tyres approach and studied a police car which cruised past, crewed with not one, but three male officers, all sharing a joke together and appearing to be blissfully underworked. The Devon and Cornwall Constabulary crest drew Hingston's attention. It was much more elaborate and frilly than the sleek, modern Metropolitan design.

Hingston tutted. 'Representative of too much time on their hands,' he muttered to himself. And then it came to him. He tapped away at his phone. The monotonous ringing became frustrating and he looked at his watch. 'Sunday!' Hingston exclaimed, realising his oversight, 'and no answerphone service,' he huffed and ended the call. He shook his head whilst he searched for the Record Office opening hours. 'Tuesday! Like living on another planet. Does *anything* ever happen down here?'

* * *

'Good morning, Plymouth and West Devon Record Office,' a cheery female chirped.

'Morning,' Hingston replied with great anticipation having waited a day and a half to make his call, 'I'm looking for a death certificate, in fact two death certificates.'

'Okay, I can assist with that,' she said.

'The first I have the details for, a Charles Embling, death registered December eighteen sixty-six.'

'Oh, you're researching the Emblings.'

Hingston remained silent in surprise.

'Very interesting. Tragic mind. You won't find a death certificate for his twin. They never found him.'

Hingston was now racing ahead of the informative Records Assistant, but every thought he tried to process was accompanied by the haunting words of the young Robert Clarke. "They didn't come home."

Chapter Six
When an Echo Speaks

"Considerable sensation was produced in the neighbourhoods of Newton St Cyres and Cadbury yesterday afternoon following the discovery of the body of a young male who had come to his death by violence near Castle Wood and rumoured to be that of Charles Embling, missing from his home some five weeks past."

Hingston speed-read the newspaper article which felt as hot off the press as those reviewed by the BBC in the tiniest hours of the morning. The calm of The Flavel library in Dartmouth had no effect on his haste and the glare of the computer screen coupled with the time-aged print scanned for modern day consumption, made his strained eyes sting.

"The body is reported to have been dead for at least three or four days. The cause of death a deep cut to the throat... an inquest on the body is expected to be held this day (Tuesday) by the city coroner, R. J. Coryndon. The police are busily engaged in making their inquiries to discover the murderer who it is hoped may be identified and brought to justice."

Hingston's heart was racing; not from his hurrying to The Flavel following his call to the Record Office, but from a sense of urgency that propelled him through the newspaper articles. His mouth was again dry and tasted of sawdust. In some respects he savoured this adrenaline rush. He felt the murder of Charles Embling was like a new case presented to him to investigate, but he knew that it may only take half an hour to review all of the newspaper headlines to reveal the murderer, the motive, the trial and the outcome of justice. Nonetheless, he was invigorated, passionately charged and enthusiastically renewed.

As he read on, the mystery of "The Castle Wood Murder" and the sensationalised morbidity of the press continued to grow. Speculation that the "cruel and barbarous" murder had been committed by Charles' "missing" twin, George, in a calculated attack likened to the biblical Cain and Abel, was printed without any consideration given to the Embling family. There was the "confession" made by a male of unsound mind which prompted what could only be described as a wild goose chase and then the arrest and trial of a Miss Eliza Norma Tolcher. Extensive blow by blow accounts were recorded about the trial which resulted in the execution of Miss Tolcher by hanging on the 6th of May 1867. The spinster was portrayed as being most unpopular in the Cadbury neighbourhood, the residents of which had "designated her for some time as a witch", not that this was considered as evidence against her, according to the papers Hingston read. Miss Tolcher was found guilty of the murder of Charles and suspected to have also murdered George, although no body or evidence of his murder was found.

Hingston felt uneasy as he reread in greater detail the circumstances of the disappearance and subsequent murder. Just like the Clarke twins, the boys appeared to have gone astray of their own volition; there was no answer as to why they left the family home one afternoon in late October 1866. There was no evidence as to where they had gone, at least not until the gruesome discovery of Charles on the 2nd of December some six miles away from home. Charles had his wrists bound with hemp rope and he had struggled wildly causing chaffing to his wrists before his throat was violently slashed, the cut "almost decapitating him". Hingston stared at the blood red wall behind the bookcases ahead of him. He diverted his eyes and saw a scarlet hexagonal stool to his right. He refocused on his computer screen and the screen saver had activated; a vivid red mass of strawberries. Hingston gasped and moved the mouse rapidly. The text reappeared, but Charles Embling read Daniel Clarke. Every reference to Charles had been replaced with Daniel and those names became blacker and bolder and darker and bigger until everything went black.

When Hingston became aware of his surroundings it was from the floor in the recovery position. An adamant Librarian maintained his position with a firm grip on his shoulder until she considered his colour had sufficiently returned and he was okay.

'We've decided not to charge you for your internet usage,' she joked. 'How are you feeling now?'

'All the better for that,' Hingston replied and sat himself up to take the glass of water offered to him. 'Thanks.'

The Librarian gave a concerned smile.

'I skipped breakfast this morning,' Hingston lied. 'I'll get something to eat in the town and then I'll be fine.'

As Hingston exited The Flavel he felt scared and alone. Blacking out was a significant deterioration in his coping mechanism or worse, a deterioration in the condition he was suffering from itself. For the first time, he realised that the decision to sign him off may have been correct and this made him shudder. Maybe pursuing an investigation into the Emblings was damaging to his health? But how could he ignore such a significant revelation when their musical box key found its way into his investigation paperwork? It would be neglect of his duties. And the substitution of the name Daniel Clarke for Charles Embling in the old newspaper text. How could that be ignored? His concern for the Clarke twins was building in his mind like an irritating itch at the base of the skull which eventually forces a person from their sleep to alleviate it. The sums were already calculated; in three days' time it would be five weeks since the Clarke twins' disappearance. Charles Embling's body was discovered five weeks after his disappearance. If Hingston's newly found fear was correct, one of the Clarke twins may imminently be murdered and based upon the events at The Flavel, that could be Daniel.

He saw Dartmouth Police Station to his left and propped himself up against the mid brown bricks, directly beneath the blue police lantern and adjacent to the blue edged glass entrance doors. The tiny, quiet station felt homely and this settled some of his anxieties. He removed his phone from his pocket, took a deep breath and dialled.

'Julia Brace,' her confident but feminine voice called out.

Her manner was unsettling. Hingston knew from countless experiences that Brace would always answer a call using the first name of the caller displayed on her phone. The only exception being for her superiors where she would address them "Sir" or "Ma'am" and change her tone from one of mild impatience; "Jason (tell me concisely)" to that of eager expectation; "Sir (I'm already onto it)".

'Ma'am, it's Jason Hingston.'

Several seconds later she spoke. 'Jason! I'm surprised to hear from you. Is everything okay?'

'Yes, ma'am. Thank you. Very briefly, I have a hunch regarding the Clarke twins.'

'Jason. You're supposed to be taking your mind off work.'

He chose to ignore this comment for responding would waste the seconds he suspected he had left of the call. 'I don't think they have gone far; possibly staying with friends or associates their parents don't know about and I've got a renewed fear for their safety.'

'Jason, you need to relax. Perhaps you should book an earlier appointment with Occupational Health as this case is clearly troubling you. Brian's managing the investigation, I can assure you.'

'By managing I presume he's keeping things ticking over. We need to increase our resources on this one, pursue enquiries with their school mates again.'

'Jason, I'll be as tactful as possible. I'm going to have to end our conversation as it is going against the recommendations of Occupational Health. I'll have to advise them that you're still troubled by this case.'

'Ma'am, with all respect, I'm really quite okay, the case is…'

'Jason, I'm sorry. I've taken your comments on board, please let the matter rest now. Take care.' The call was cut.

Hingston was stressed. He pressed his hand against the rough brickwork of the police station which had been warmed by the sun and levered himself off the wall to walk through the car park in the direction of the river. To his relief the chimes began to play.

He continued past an array of art galleries and tried to take his thoughts away from the Clarke twins and Brace by stopping at every window. There were scenes like those he enjoyed at Salcombe; estuary views, sandy coves and colourful sails, all splashed with lashings of oil paint. There were childlike pen and ink rows of seaside objects, expertly detailed Devonshire hills and then his cotton shirt became subject of the inartistic attentions of a seagull.

'Bloody hell!' Hingston held his shirt sleeve away from his body in disgust.

A few shops down, two ten-year-old girls had noticed the commotion and were giggling uncontrollably behind their hands as Hingston now headed to Uncle Zack's.

* * *

As he opened the front door a flash of apprehension struck his upper chest and he paused instinctively. The tune of the musical box was chiming. He pulled the door back towards him. The music was muffled; it was not playing in his mind, it was inside the house. Hingston stepped back and scanned the windows of the pale blue Victorian terrace. No signs of forced entry; no visible movement inside; curtain positions unchanged from earlier. He pushed the door back open, stepped into the hallway and checked his line of sight into each room and up the stairs to where the music continued to chime. He reached for Uncle Zack's golfing umbrella and ascended the stairs, keeping to the left to minimise the creaking and cracking of the old wood. The sun streamed from Hingston's room on the left of the landing and lit the carpet in the upstairs hallway. He held the umbrella in his right hand, a third of the way down its length, thought about how many years it had been since he was in uniform and suddenly felt very bare without his public protection equipment. The music came to a gentle stop and he paused, one step from the landing. The silence was as intense as the brilliant sunlight on the cream carpet. He strained to hear any movement. He glanced across the hall; the door to the bathroom was ajar and the other two bedrooms were closed. The sunlight on the carpet went out.

'Police!' he bellowed and darted onto the landing, positioning himself away from the danger of the staircase, umbrella held in front with both hands.

'Jason! What's the matter? You trying to give me a heart attack?' Uncle Zack laughed. 'Give us that umbrella!'

'Finding someone in the house unannounced and playing that musical box is what's the matter!' Hingston rolled his eyes as he threw the umbrella Fred Astair style into Uncle Zack's outspread hand.

'Well, I did call as I had promised, but you were obviously out of the house *and* somewhere without a signal,' Zack said. 'Very nice musical box. Saw it on the side there and felt compelled to give it a go. Where did you get it from? Surely not Dartmouth? Haven't seen antiques like that round here.'

'No, Totnes.' Hingston continued the conversation as they walked downstairs to shut the front door and he began to laugh about the palaver he had got himself into since the gull had struck. 'Look at the bloody state I'm in,' he said, presenting his arm to Uncle Zack.

'Oh! Three strikes you're out, my boy,' Zack joked. 'Baseball's on Sky tonight if you're interested?'

* * *

The crisp, heavy table linen in white and burgundy offset the earthy tones and jewel inspired colours in the bowls of curries and rice as they were placed in considerable number between Hingston and Uncle Zack. They had a window seat in the restaurant and the royal spread of delights was well earned because the pair had put in an afternoon of hard graft on the kitchen. The small talk was long over, as was the account of Aunt Beryl's broken leg and her associated grumpiness.

'So tell me, Jason, got any exciting news? Any plans of settling down yet?' Uncle Zack probed with great anticipation in his voice.

Hingston wondered whether his dad had said something to prompt this question. 'Let's see,' Hingston paused, 'I've been Detective Sergeant for two and a half years; love the job; the time passes very quickly. It's very demanding, but it's a good team and we get some very good results. Got the house just as I want it now.'

Uncle Zack gave an expectant look and nodded his head.

'No exciting news in the respect you're enquiring about!' Hingston laughed. 'Don't have a lot of time outside of work, to be fair.'

'Well you're on holiday now,' Zack spooned a mound of rice onto his plate and reached for the chicken madras. 'Except you're sat here on a quiet Tuesday night, in an almost deserted restaurant with an old bloke! You're not young forever you know. Look at me; sixty-two and never got married. Too busy pursuing other interests. You'll be a lonely old detective before you know it, Jason.'

Hingston stopped himself from complaining, tried to push memories of Remi to the back of his mind and redirected the conversation. 'Talking of women, and I'm not meaning the young or the good looking, have you ever come across the old dear who lives near Bayard's Cove Fort?'

'I've never seen myself as a toy boy, Jason, no!' he teased.

Hingston shook his head. 'Seriously. It's hard to put an age on her; at least mid-eighties I'd say. Only about five foot two, grey bun, dreary dress sense and has a carved stick. Quite a busybody. Says she's a regular visitor of Bayard's Cove.'

'No,' Uncle Zack pondered the description. 'Can't say she's ringing any bells. Why d'you ask? What's the interest?'

'I've bumped into her a couple of times since I arrived, or rather she's bumped into me.'

'I wouldn't be too concerned about an eighty-five-year-old stalking you, Jason,' Uncle Zack winked. 'We really don't get crime down here, you know.' He snapped a shard off a poppadom and ate it noisily with a smile.

'I'll have to challenge that comment,' Hingston replied with an air of superiority. 'First of all, the elderly woman disagrees with that blinkered misconception with great conviction, and secondly, I've been reading about the murder of a boy that happened at Castle Wood in Cadbury. Now, this old woman…'

'Hang about, why were you reading about a murder at Castle Wood? When did this happen?'

'Eighteen sixty-six.'

'Eighteen sixty-six!' Zack interrupted. 'Now, this is familiar,' he tapped his index and middle fingers on the table cloth. 'I've heard of this murder… yes, Embling! Boy's name was Embling.'

'Yes!' Jason's stare was flooded with astonishment at his uncle's breadth of knowledge of local history.

'What are you doing looking up historic murders in Devon? Don't you get enough about murders at work?'

'Hey, I was just about to tell you if you hold your horses for a moment,' Hingston scolded in jest. 'That musical box I bought belonged to the Embling family.'

Uncle Zack began to frown.

'Inside the musical box is a handkerchief which was embroidered by an Elizabeth Embling in eighteen sixty.' Hingston secured a nod from Zack. 'Embroidered in the centre is a verse from Proverbs which relates to children and around the embroidered border are six names. I deduced these were her six children.'

'Okay,' he confirmed.

'I had an inkling they were from the Exeter region because there's a piece of newspaper also inside the box which suggested this would be the case. An online birth record search supported my belief and having telephoned the local Record Office this morning it was confirmed that two of Elizabeth's children were twin boys; both went missing and one was found murdered.'

Uncle Zack shook his head. 'My word, Jason. What a find! I know a few historians from Exeter. Met them at Uni. They'd be fascinated. But how much did this musical box cost you? What made you buy it?'

'Ha! This is where it starts to get a bit weird. Let's say keep an open mind on this one,' Hingston smiled. 'I paid forty quid for it.'

'Forty? That's got to be worth a few thousand, easy.'

'It was in a bric-a-brac shop, full of a load of junk. I mean *real* junk. And amongst it was this box and it was locked. The owner said it had been there for donkey's years, locked the whole time. She thought it had come from a school science lab. She clearly had no idea it was a musical box.'

'But I saw the key on the bedside cabinet, Jason.'

'Yes. That's why it's so weird. I already had the key.'

'What? How on earth?'

Hingston leaned across the table, looked Uncle Zack in the eye and paused with an apprehensive expression. 'It appeared within a stack of paperwork on my desk at Chiswick Police Station.'

'You serious? Or are you pulling my leg?' Uncle Zack returned Hingston's worried look.

'The paperwork that relates to my investigation into missing twin boys,' Hingston whispered.

Uncle Zack slammed the palm of his hand onto the edge of the table making an almighty crash as the bowls and cutlery shook. 'That's more than a bit weird, my boy, it's spooky. What do you make of it all? Don't you think it's spooky?'

'Yes, but there's got to be a reason for it all; the appearance of the key, the discovery of the box and the parallel that seems to exist between both sets of twins.'

Uncle Zack shook his head again. 'The chances of you coming down here for your holiday and finding that box. In fact, what luck you even *had* a holiday the way you work yourself!' he exclaimed.

'Yes,' Hingston pursed his lips and felt a swathe of guilt pass over him. 'I was intentionally brief when I called you last Thursday and shouldn't have been. I'm on leave from work, but it's classed as sick leave; I've been signed off.'

'Jason, my boy, why has this happened? What's up?'

'I haven't been sleeping properly,' Hingston said.

'Well, no surprise with a job like yours; too much stress and a shift pattern to boot,' he defended his nephew reactively. Zack's fork had been rested on his plate for a good couple of minutes and there was no indication he realised his curry was beginning to cool.

'There's more to it. I've been suffering from what's called night terrors. I wake up in a right state, but can't remember exactly what I dreamt that set me off. There's only a few snippets I can recall.'

Uncle Zack appeared very concerned.

'Occupational Health have concluded it's anxiety and insufficient rest.'

'And what do you think? Do you agree?'

'There's an additional factor that Occupational Health deemed to be an hallucination; after the night terrors I hear music, it's really *there* in the room as far as I can tell, but it makes me relax and recover. They had no other answer for it. I didn't really know what to make of it all, but *now* after this key has appeared...' Hingston stared at Uncle Zack.

'It's all right, Jason, you can tell me. Go on.'

'The music that was deemed an hallucination is the *same* music that plays from the musical box. Not the whole piece, but some of the bars.' Hingston's voice began to pick up pace. 'I *knew* that music very well before I ever knew of the box. And, to top it all off, these night terrors started *after* I was assigned to investigate the missing twins. And now there's this uncanny link between my investigation and the past; the main tangible connection being the box and the fate of the previous owners.'

'Jason, slow down. I can barely keep up.' Inwardly, Zack began to fear for his nephew's sanity.

Hingston inhaled and touched his head. 'It's madness.' He scanned Uncle Zack's wide blue eyes and puckered brow and mirrored his expression of disbelief. 'What am I seeing in these night terrors that I can't remember? Why is this happening to me and what am I supposed to be doing about it? The past few days have set my head spinning with questions,' Hingston appealed to Uncle Zack with open palms for a solution.

'We Hingstons aren't superstitious, Jason, I don't have to tell you that. But it feels like there's a reason you have found out about this murder from the past. You're a superb detective, my boy. Do what you do best; find the solution.' Uncle Zack gave a concerned, but encouraging smile.

'The bloody system is against me now that I'm signed off,' Hingston protested. 'I'm concerned about the twins, so I phone my DI and what does she do?'

'Nothing?'

'That's politer than I would've put it, Uncle Zack. It's like you're signed off and therefore mentally unstable! Incapable of logical thought!' Hingston realised his frustration was increasing his volume of speech. He glanced across the restaurant and lowered his voice. 'By the time I get back it could be too late.'

'Then prove you're well and get back sooner, my boy!'

'If I tell them what I've told you, they'll probably think I've flipped. I've got to play this carefully.' Hingston looked out through the multi-pane window of the first floor restaurant and peered down at the street below. The evening had remained warm, but now it was dark the passersby were few. The street lamps imbued the shop fronts with a rich saffron hue. 'There she is!' Hingston called out.

'Who?'

'The old dear from Bayard's Cove. Look!'

Uncle Zack stood up and leant across the table. He huffed, 'Can't see out from here,' and moved to Hingston's window. 'Whereabouts? Where is she?'

Hingston pointed. 'There, going in the direction of the fort.'

'Oh, yes. She blends in rather well in the dark. Grey bun's a tad old fashioned. Looks doddery with that stick.' Uncle Zack was relieved she was real and not a figment of Hingston's imagination.

And then she disappeared from view.

'I was going to tell you about her before we got onto the Castle Wood murder.'

Uncle Zack returned to his seat and they began to tuck into their meal once more.

'I've spoken with her twice,' Hingston said. 'Both occasions she has caught me by surprise and she seems to possess a preternatural ability to judge me, possibly even my thoughts. At Bayard's Cove, I left her in the fort for less than a couple of minutes and then returned. I'm sure I could hear her singing, but she'd gone. There's no way she could have got past me. It's illogical.'

'Mmmm?' Uncle Zack mumbled through his madras with a perplexed expression on display.

Hingston took a bite of an onion bhaji. 'You see...' he chewed a few times and swallowed hard. 'At our first meeting she was referring to my "problem".' He ate some more of his bhaji.

'It's very common for people to have problems. Perhaps that's a line she uses all the time? A conversation starter?' Uncle Zack suggested.

'Maybe, if you take that in isolation, but she's insistent that to solve my problem I need to keep an open mind and that I shouldn't hide from my fears.'

'Mmmm,' Uncle Zack nodded as he finished his mouthful. 'Interesting. It's pretty sound advice for solving any problem, but in the context of the issues you're dealing with, your police investigation, the night terrors and all this funny goings on, I suppose it's ringing true to some extent.'

Hingston nodded in response.

'You know there are some odd folk down here, bit into the psychic, magical, fairy stuff. Perhaps she's one of those,' Uncle Zack continued.

'Yes, I got my head round that concept when I visited Totnes.'

'Perhaps, my boy, you should listen to her advice and first and foremost contact that DI of yours and get her to listen up!' Uncle Zack rose from his seat. 'Give us a minute,' he said and headed to the gents.

Hingston turned his attention back to the street below. The saffron lighting appeared more vibrant now that the sun had fully set. There, within the light of the nearest lamp which cast a wide glow upon the pavement, he could make out the shape of the curly haired boy who was running within that spot of light like a cine film playing over and over. Hingston saw the motion of the long grass swaying in the breeze and flowing either side of the boy as he parted the tendril-like blades and fluffy seed heads, and this entranced Hingston all the more as he continued to stare. The boy's curls and braces came into focus and Hingston almost felt the urge to run out of the restaurant to try to catch him up.

'Still haven't finished that bhaji, then,' Uncle Zack boomed as he returned to his seat.

Hingston spun his head back round, shaken from his deep concentration. 'Er, no, not quite,' he replied and regained his sight of the street lamp. Looking back at him was the old woman, stood in the exact spot the boy had been running. Hingston blinked. 'I think I've eaten just about enough for tonight,' he added and watched as the elderly woman moved out of the light and walked once again in the direction of Bayard's Cove.

Chapter Seven
A Game of Two Halves

Over the next two days Hingston stepped up his activity to pursue coastal walks at Blackpool Sands and Salcombe. He fitted the new cabinets in the kitchen and took a couple of strolls to Bayard's Cove, half expecting, half hoping to meet the elderly woman, but since her appearance beneath the street light she was impossible to find. This troubled Hingston, making him feel compelled to speak with her. Why did she stand there, gazing up at him, expressionless, through the restaurant window? How had she even come to notice him there?

Uncle Zack had been supportive and non-judgemental. Hingston knew the occurrence of his night terrors would not have left Zack undisturbed, nor would the magnificent acoustics of the musical box have been dulled sufficiently by the closed bedroom door, but he quietly understood and made no mention of it.

Thursday afternoon Hingston took a solitary ten-minute drive around the coast and parked up in the sloping concreted area nestled aside the rugged cliffs at Blackpool Sands. The £4 entrance fee was worth every penny the moment he walked to the front of the beach shop and onto the expanse of pebbles. The sea sparkled and small foaming waves bowed in appreciation over the glistening smooth stones and sand; the perfect stage within a natural amphitheatre of fiery slate cliffs and luscious plant life. Hingston trudged through the deep hoards of pebbles, inhaled and savoured the salty air and listened to the hypnotic mantra of the sea whilst he made his way to a large boulder at stage right of the cove. Here he pondered the old woman's advice, hoping he may find a path through the labyrinth in his mind.

As Hingston scanned the horizon which was as vast and open and as full of the unknown as his case investigation, he reached down to his right and ran his hand through the hot baked pebbles. He found a flat, smooth piece of blue-grey sedimentary stone and rubbed it between his fingers. It was pleasingly tactile. The warmth radiated and its surface cooled. He glanced back at the beach and noticed several more of these irregularly sized, wobbly edged pieces of stone which he collected up to form a stack. They struck against each other making mellow clinking sounds as they slid about in his hands. He stepped down towards the lapping frothy waves and skimmed the first stone into the sea; *chhhup, chuup* and a silent plop as it was engulfed. He slid the next off the top of the stack and repeated; he got three bounces that time. With each stone thereafter he discarded a fear therapeutically into the expanse. He knew that those fears, like the stones themselves, would not be carried away forever by the tide, but it served as a stress relief. Along with the slate medallions plunged the images of his last day in the office: *chhhup, chuup*, a serious Brace with her arms rested calmly on her desk, her frown lines activated in managerial concern between her dove grey eyes; *chhhup, chhup, chuup*, the twisted phone cord and the loops he had created along it which mimicked his knotted stomach; *chhhup, chuup*, the words "Best Detective" which made him feel so inadequate; *chhhup, chuup*, the handing over of his investigation; *chhhup, chhup, chuup,* the...

He paused, stone in hand. 'The key,' he said out loud. His words bounced through his brain like the skimming stones on the water. The elderly woman's words suddenly began to mean so much more. "Keep an open mind and let your thoughts ebb and flow like the sea. That is the *key* to solving your problem." And again,

"Hiding from your fears is certainly not the *key* to solving your problem".

The night terrors made him fearful. So did the mass of unanswered questions in the Clarke twins' case. The Embling twins' case, the appearance of the key and musical box made him even more *fearful*. And then, that was it. He considered something differently for the first time. Was the old woman telling him to face all of these fears and that the physical key to the musical box will provide the solution? The enormity of this possibility filled his whole body and seeped out through his pores. Hingston stared at the waves for several minutes in a trance-like state. He *had* to see her again.

Almost twenty-four hours later and now on the Championship Course of the Dartmouth Golf and Country Club, Hingston and Zack strode across the glorious green landscape with electric golf trolleys leading the way. The winding streams and showy fountains added panache to the immaculate, groomed oasis which blossomed amidst far reaching flourishing fields. An azure blue sky intensified the beauty of the bejewelled countryside and Hingston breathed deeply the fresh sea air drifting in from the coast.

Uncle Zack prepared to take his next putt.

Whilst the morning had served as an exhilarating and refreshing escape, the afternoon was now beginning to be eaten away by Hingston's worries. He thought about the elderly woman. He wanted to ask her some direct questions.

Hingston's phone rang briefly and then cut out as the signal was lost.

'You trying to put me off?' Uncle Zack laughed, ''Cause it ain't gonna work!'

Hingston was frowning at his phone.

'You all right, my boy? Something wrong?'

'Yeah,' Hingston replied and continued to frown. He tapped at his phone to display the missed calls register.

Uncle Zack paused, looking at Hingston rather than his golf ball.

'Mmmm?' Hingston seemed surprised. 'It was Rob. From the office. He's one of my DCs.'

'You're not going to get a successful call from him here,' Uncle Zack advised. 'That's why this course is more popular than the local fishing; best place to get away from the wife!' he laughed.

Hingston was not paying a great deal of attention as he raised his phone to his ear. 'Damn. No signal,' Hingston complained. He wandered around the green waving his phone and checking his signal bar obsessively.

Uncle Zack stood, waiting to resume his shot.

A shrill beeping noise signalled that a voice message had been received. Hingston went straight to it, but the signal was very poor and the message faded in and out. 'Sarge, it… call, but… Clarke… a.m. this morning… otid artery… king kicked off… way murder squad are onto it… me. Cheers.'

And the game came to an abrupt and premature end.

Chapter Eight
Anchors Aweigh

The murder of Daniel Clarke was national news by six p.m. that evening. Of course his name was not released, despite his parents' positive identification; the results of the post mortem first had to be received.

'Police are appealing for witnesses following the discovery of the body of a teenage boy who was found in the early hours of this morning in Burlington Park, Chiswick. A murder investigation has been launched and is in its early stages. A police spokesperson confirmed that the boy had received stab wounds, however, the results of the post mortem which will establish the cause of death are still awaited at this time.'

Hingston turned off the television and picked up his jacket. 'Just off for a walk,' he called to Uncle Zack who was working on the tiling in the kitchen.

'Okay, my boy. Grab us a takeaway on your way back.'

'Will do.' Hingston closed the front door behind him.

The image of the sunny entrance to Burlington Park with two sombre, stocky, male officers stood guard wearing their bulky black body armour, traditional custodian helmets and crisp white shirts remained with him as he walked to the quayside. The details of Daniel's murder, withheld from the public, but later shared by Rob over the phone, played round in his mind.

Daniel had been stabbed in the neck three times. The professional opinion from the scene being that one of the wounds had severed his carotid artery causing him to bleed to death. Memories of the newspapers read in The Flavel library competed with this description. The substitution of the name Daniel Clarke for Charles Embling replayed in his mind, forcing him to find the nearest bench and sit down with his head between his knees. He recalled his compulsion to telephone Brace who brushed aside his concerns for the safety of the Clarke twins, and who he suspected had not even taken his comments on board. He tried to concentrate on the new information supplied by Rob.

Daniel had been found by a shift worker who was walking his dog at three a.m. this morning. Daniel had no clothing on his upper body and was wearing only his black school trousers and trainers; presumably those from his P.E. kit which he had taken to school on Friday the 15th of April. He was laying on his front and was slumped towards a laurel bush as though the murderer had attempted to drag him into the bush to conceal him, but for whatever reason gave up before getting him there.

Everyone is well educated in the capacity of modern forensic science thanks to the countless crime series and documentaries which provide fascinating viewing for the innocent, but a pernicious education for those who plot a crime aiming to evade scientific techniques. Perhaps the upper clothing was removed for that very reason; to take away the material which may have revealed the murderer's own DNA. If Daniel was stabbed in the neck three times, he could have fought back after the first and possibly second wound, before the fatal wound was inflicted. Unlike Charles Embling, his wrists were not bound. But he *was* murdered by a knife attack to the throat.

Hingston opened his eyes, gazed at the biscuit coloured paving slabs and lifted his head to stare out across the River Dart. It was now half past six. In an hour and a half he would be setting off for London, back to his suburban semi to embark on his own investigation. It mattered not whether Brace approved or believed him or thought he was unwell and off kilter, because she would know nothing about it until the timing was just right.

'Bollocks to Brace!' he thought and strode to Bayard's Cove. He stepped under the rugged asymmetrical arch, surveyed the empty fort and listened for the notes of a seaside ditty sung or hummed faintly against the sounds of the river and the passing gulls. He paced across the flagstones and confirmed he was alone. It was only a week ago he met her here for the first time, but it felt so much longer. He glanced across the gunports again, convinced he could feel her presence, but perhaps that was only due to his own indomitable pursuit of her.

Four houses down from the fort was "The Lookout"; its soft lemon paintwork glowed in the early evening light. The lace doily beneath the fruit bowl was as immaculate as before. He stood outside the front door and scanned the windows for movement. All appeared quiet, but he was not dissuaded from reaching toward the doorbell.

'I don't answer the bell,' her familiar voice interrupted before Hingston's index finger touched the cast iron button.

He jumped, having not noticed her advance.

'I wouldn't have let you in either, even if I knew you were coming.'

Hingston began to find her obstructive manner irritating and felt bubbles of annoyance begin to surface and simmer alongside his frustration with Brace. 'I've come to see you, madam.' He paused and controlled his tone. 'Firstly, to say thank you for your advice.' Again he paused, this time for his words to register with the elderly woman and to observe her response.

A very faint smile passed across her lips and she continued to stare at him.

Hingston noticed that she wore the same clothes, walked with the same stick and her hair was fashioned in the same style bun. He also noticed for the first time, that she did not carry a handbag or a purse and his eyes were drawn to the low pockets in her long, baggy, navy cardigan as he searched for signs of a house key within them.

She pulled her cardigan around her with her wrinkled left hand and maintained a firm grip on her stick with the other. 'Perhaps we could sit down on that bench,' she instructed rather than suggested and began to walk towards it, denying Hingston a view of her cardigan pockets.

He followed and they sat facing the river with the townhouse behind them.

'You wanted to thank me for my advice?' the elderly woman questioned in a self-appreciating manner.

Hingston stared back at her sunken eyes. He ignored her prompt for him to thank her for a second time and pushed ahead. 'And to ask you what it is about me and my "problem" that interests you so much.'

She laughed softly. 'You have read a lot into my advice, I see!'

Hingston remained silent, forcing her to speak.

'I'm gratified to learn that you have identified your problem. But that is it; it is *your* problem and the key to solving it lies with you,' she smiled.

'Madam, please, you haven't answered my question.'

'You're not awfully keen on answering mine as I recall,' she retorted with some vigour.

Hingston swallowed as he does in Custody when he's allowed his detainee to control the content of the interview for long enough and it's apparent they will not provide anything more than waffle, unless directed. 'On Tuesday evening were you stood under the streetlight on Lower Street looking up at me in the Indian restaurant?'

'Well, yes. You saw me didn't you?' she replied with a cheekiness Hingston was not expecting, but which he ignored.

'Why was that?'

'A reminder,' she stated with such simplicity it was as if he need not have asked, for surely it was obvious.

If it had only been the old woman he had seen, then her response would have been straightforward and acceptable; a reminder of herself and what she had told him. But that was not the case. Seconds before, under the same saffron glow, the curly haired boy had been running interminably through his grassy meadow. And then *her*; looking him coldly in the eye, just as she was doing now.

'A reminder of what?' he probed.

'A reminder is a personal thing; only the person who receives the reminder understands its full meaning, and again that brings it back to you,' she smiled. 'Presumably it had some effect otherwise why would you have been about to ring that doorbell?' The elderly woman gained control of the exchange with stealthy expertise.

Hingston felt a peculiar sensation, not dissimilar to déjà vu, for he found himself at the beginning of his conversation again, ready to explain why he had come to see her.

In the moment he pondered this feeling, the elderly woman had risen to her feet, leaning heavily on her stick. 'It's nice to be appreciated,' she added. 'Maybe when you're a little nearer to solving your problem we could have another tête-à-tête.'

'So you *are* interested?' Hingston attempted to catch her out.

She began to walk away, past "The Lookout" and down to Bayard's Cove Fort.

Hingston called after her, 'Who is the boy?'

After several yards she paused, just as she had done before, and her voice carried on the air. 'Keep an open mind and let your thoughts ebb and flow like the sea,' she said and walked away.

Hingston completed her sentence in his mind and only then considered the context in which she may have applied its meaning this evening. Her response was typically ambiguous. As he pondered, he remembered the direct reference she made to the key this evening. "It is *your* problem and the *key* to solving it lies with you."

'She *is* referring to the musical box,' Hingston decided. He knew the elderly woman would not tell him *anything* unless she wanted to, but he was not prepared to let this opportunity pass. He rose from the bench to hurry after her. "The Lookout" now had a light on in one of the windows and he was distracted by it.

He looked back towards the elderly woman and she had disappeared! He jogged along the cobbles in disbelief feeling annoyed and sick with nervousness. How could she leave him without a sound explanation when he was returning to London tonight?

'You are a persistent sort,' she laughed, catching him off guard as she stepped into his line of sight in the centre of the fort.

Hingston moved towards her. 'Please, tell me what you know.'

'The ebb and flow of the sea is reliable, but it has no measure of time. It cannot be hurried, but it will not be stopped. An open mind worries not about time because life *is* a continuous ebb and flow. The answers you are seeking will surface like polished pebbles returning to a beach. When they do, *you will* solve your problem, but they will only come when *they* are ready.'

* * *

'You drive safely, Jason,' Uncle Zack insisted. 'I know what you coppers are like for speeding on an open road.'

'I'm not about to add a road traffic offence and an internal investigation to my list of worries!' Hingston laughed, his showmanship appeal returning fleetingly.

'Seriously, Jason, what I was saying over dinner; anything you need, any time, let me know. And make sure you visit again soon. *Before* they get you back to that grindstone. We've got a game of golf to play!'

Hingston patted Uncle Zack on the back and felt slightly sad. 'Will do, on both counts,' he reassured him.

'You got that musical box packed securely? It's not gonna break is it?'

'Yes, well wrapped, inside a cardboard box of yours and wedged behind the passenger seat. See, I'm even taking your rubbish away with me!'

Zack chortled as Hingston walked round to the driver's door. 'Thanks for your help on the kitchen.'

'Told you I didn't take after Dad,' Hingston smiled as he sat in the car and shut the door with a loud clunk. He turned the ignition and wound down the passenger window which enabled Zack to pop his head inside instead of pressing his face up against the glass.

'Good luck for tomorrow,' he added, slapped the roof of the car and stepped back onto the kerb to wave Hingston off into the warm Friday evening.

Chapter Nine
Saturday, 21st of May

A small gaggle of Canada geese honked on the sunlit, geometric lake. A couple of studious early birds stood by the imposing glass entrance doors and at one minute to opening time Hingston buzzed with anticipation as he controlled his stride to avoid springing into a jog. The smooth, modernistic concrete and glass buildings reflected in the still lake and the grandiose soft grey granite paving exuded a Zen-like calm which was perfect for a day's studying. For Hingston, his adrenaline rush would not subside until he was seated within these peaceful walls that housed The National Archives.

Ahead of the staircase, just past the petite, crammed bookshop, Hingston made a point of overtaking the two early birds he had met at the entrance. The bookshop was an Aladdin's cave where bindings galore were positioned on dark wooden shelves and eye-catching displays of the newest titles were placed strategically to entice researchers and historians to stop by and investigate the written works of other researchers and historians. At nine a.m. sharp on a Saturday morning, however, it failed to distract Hingston and the early birds from the purpose of their visits. There was, of course, no real need for Hingston to make such an effort to beat the other two men to the computer room upstairs, but having driven back from Dartmouth especially, he wanted the sense of satisfaction that he had maximised his day of investigation at Kew.

His reader's ticket was due to expire in one month. He last visited The National Archives when he was researching a relative who was a conscientious objector in 1916. The purpose of his visit today would take him back a further fifty years and in only twenty minutes from submitting his request from the computer room, he would be placing his fingers on the police records of Charles Embling's murder investigation.

Hingston found himself a seat near the window in the reading room from where he had superb lighting and he could look across the empty tables and chairs to the lockers where his awaited file would be placed. It was like a surveillance operation; eyes fixed on the target. His mind, of course, had a second focus; the Clarke twins. In the coming hours Daniel's name will be broadcast to the country. The announcement and the public response shall be captured by the press and archived for historical preservation, just as was done for Charles Embling's murder so many years ago. A huge swathe of floral tributes will pile up at the entrance to Burlington Park and they shall lay there sacrificially to slowly join Daniel in death.

Speculation about the fate of Nathan Clarke will soon be voiced with an acceptable amount of pessimism. Nathan, if still alive, will be beside himself with fear and desperation. Did he witness the murder of his twin? Where is he and why has he still not been found? Hingston wanted answers and he needed them for the Clarke family. Maybe today, reading the Victorian police investigation file he will identify how to obtain them.

Before long, he saw a well presented middle aged woman walk across to the lockers with a file in her hand. He made his way to the glossy, red Perspex fronted lockers with the impatience of a child on Christmas morning; no sooner had the woman deposited the wrapped bundle, Hingston dived straight in to retrieve it.

* * *

The reading room was silent and Hingston sat in solitude within it. He held back so as to savour the motion of opening the file's cover which would plunge him into the world of Victorian policing. It was exactly nine thirty when his eyes met the first mid blue sheet of paper which lay at the top of an inch and a half thick stack. Before he read the content, he acclimatised himself to the pristine, calligraphic handwriting which was as uniformed as typed script but far more beautiful and expressive. Flamboyant, flowing capital letters embellished the page which was scribed with passion and respect for the English language, the seriousness of the policing matter in hand and for the ultimate recipient of the letter, the Metropolitan Police Commissioner, Scotland Yard. The letter itself was addressed to the Metropolitan Police Detective Department and was dated the 5th of December 1866.

The handwriting spanned two thirds of the width of the page, leaving a chunky, regimentally straight margin, which reflected the discipline of the writer. Hingston gently lifted the first page of the letter which was numbered and turned to the sixth and final page where the signature read "Bell" and underneath, his title, "Inspector". He returned the first five pages to the top of the stack and began to read the account of Inspector Bell with as much anticipation and intrigue as his detective predecessors would have felt in 1866.

Upon Inspector Bell's arrival at the parish of Cadbury he was briefed by the local police on their investigation over the past three days since the discovery of the body. The body, identified as that of Charles Embling on Tuesday the 4th of December, had been found by a local farm labourer who was walking along the perimeter of Castle Wood following morning church service on Sunday the 2nd of December. The body had been left in deep undergrowth, face down, head turned to the left, hands tied with hemp rope behind his back. It appeared the murderer had bound Charles' wrists tightly, but excessive struggling had loosened the rope sufficiently to cause bruising and open grazes prior to his throat being deeply cut. The city coroner had concluded that Charles was bound for at least half an hour before his life was taken. There was no evidence the body had been moved. It was surmised that his throat had been cut whilst the murderer stood behind him, who then simply allowed the boy's body to drop into the undergrowth. No attempt to conceal the body had been made. An estimated three or four days had passed before the body was discovered. Local police had searched the surrounding area extensively for the weapon, but to no avail.

On Monday the 3rd of December, local Constable Heale was approached by a woman from the parish who alleged she had witnessed "the spinster", a Miss Tolcher, who she described as a "heathen" and a "practiser of strange and ungodly ways", performing "something of question which inspired fear in my very soul" at the site of Charles' murder. She herself had walked to Castle Wood "to pray for the soul of the dear boy" at eight-o-clock that morning and upon arrival witnessed the practices of Miss Tolcher which prompted her to report her suspicion to Constable Heale right away; her suspicion that Miss Tolcher had sacrificed the boy to the Devil.

Constable Heale set to the site of the murder and observed a number of acorns and a branch of holly laid across the ground where the body had been found. Miss Tolcher was not present. He therefore returned to the parish and attended Miss Tolcher's home where he spoke with her at length. She denied any involvement in the murder and defended her visit to Castle Wood as "nowt more than respect given". There was no evidence to suspect Miss Tolcher had any involvement in the murder.

Inspector Bell was thorough in his account. He reported that the father of Charles Embling, a Mr Richard Embling, who was a "notable gentleman" of Newton St Cyres, had requested the scientific examination of his son's retinas in pursuit of the photographic image of his final sight of the world, in the hope this would reveal the identity of the murderer. It was explained to Mr Embling that such a science would only apply if the body had been discovered much sooner after death and that his son's field of vision would have been largely obscured by the undergrowth.

Hingston paused at this point to contemplate what must have been one of the earliest forms of forensic science, albeit a leap in the wrong direction which undoubtedly would have caused great disappointment to Victorian crime fighters and seekers of justice when it was proven that retina memory was not scientific fact.

Inspector Bell's letter continued with a profound sense of urgency. Impressively, on the day of the 5th of December, the day of writing his letter, Inspector Bell visited the murder scene and made enquiries with a third of the residents of the parish, including Miss Tolcher, which totalled sixty-eight persons. However, he found no witnesses to the murder, no persons who had seen Charles Embling or his twin, George, and no persons who gave information which he considered would lead to the identification of the murderer or who gave rise to suspicion of involvement in the murder. Not even Miss Tolcher. However, he noted that Miss Tolcher had, twelve years ago, been imprisoned for theft of potatoes. Additionally, two women within the parish who having heard of the accusation made against Miss Tolcher on the 3rd of December voiced their opinions that Miss Tolcher was indeed as "heathen" as reported.

In swift conclusion, Inspector Bell committed himself to another day of thorough investigation in which "every enquiry will be made and every means will be used to identify the murderer".

Hingston inhaled deeply as he revealed the second document which was again penned by Inspector Bell in his structured, gentlemanly tone. "I beg to report on the ninth of December a blacksmith named Henry Cole attended the Parish Church of St Cyr and St Julitta, Newton St Cyres, for morning service as he did attend regularly as a parishioner. Present were Mr Richard Embling, his wife Elizabeth and their children, who as devout Christians maintained their attendance at church despite their great pain and suffering. In a sudden outburst, described by the vicar as a scream of hysteria, Henry Cole rose from the pew and begged for mercy from the Almighty. The congregation remained silent as Henry Cole confessed to the murder of Charles Embling before alighting from the church. Mrs Embling collapsed within moments of the shocking announcement and the service was abruptly ended with several of the younger men from the congregation pursuing Henry Cole and swiftly capturing him a short distance from the Vicarage."

Hingston thought back to the newspaper accounts he read in The Flavel library and remembered the male of unsound mind who had confessed to the murder. He skimmed through the remainder of Inspector Bell's letter which most definitely was the start of a wild goose chase, for Hingston was more concerned about what had occurred *afterwards* that lead to the hanging of Miss Tolcher. It seemed strange that the early investigation had discounted Miss Tolcher not once, but twice; the local police and Inspector Bell had no evidence or professional suspicion to cast doubt upon the integrity of Miss Tolcher, at least nothing more incriminating than some pagan practices and a one-off potato theft.

He continued to leaf through Inspector Bell's paperwork. Scattered between the blue sheets were golden aged newspaper cuttings, some of which he had viewed electronically at The Flavel. He smiled as he came across an "Extraordinary Expenses" claim form which was a printed document, red font on blue paper, where Inspector Bell completed the blanks to indicate that his expenses were "necessarily incurred beyond the limits of the Police District" in order to make enquiries respecting the Castle Wood murder. Hingston realised that Inspector Bell had been loaned to the local police force from the Metropolitan Police due to his specialist detective skills. A detailed list of Inspector Bell's refreshments and travel costs were recorded with impeccable neatness including the respective distances travelled by cab, rail and dog cart. The financial breakdown of each item was displayed in pounds, shillings and pence. The Chief Clerk endorsed the claim which totalled a substantial seven pounds, eight shillings and tuppence by recording "murder the special circumstances of the case".

Beneath the claim form lay numerous documents associated with Henry Cole. Hingston maintained a steady pace as his sense of impatience began to build and his breathing became shallower and faster. As last: something new. Hingston picked up an irregularly sized piece of paper which was somewhere between A4 and A5 size, soft grey in colour and covered with large, scratchy handwriting which was scrawled across the page with two final lines squeezed vertically down the narrow margin. The letter had been folded down the centre by its author, but since its receipt it had been kept open to prevent the flimsy paper from becoming further damaged by the crease. Hingston tilted the page into the light of the window and strained to make out the text.

"Sir. I urge you humbly to consider who be the murderer of the boy in the wood. Have you searched the cave of the heathen woman? She secretly visits this place of evil. Pray find her hiding place and find her guilty. Tis hidden in the wood. Your humble servant, a man. J.B."

Hingston stared at this anonymous note and wondered whether "J.B." was ever identified, for clearly this was the start; the moment in which the investigation was directed again at Miss Tolcher and where the finger of blame remained, but why? The answer was soon to unfold within another letter from Inspector Bell dated the 16th of December 1866.

The pace at which Hingston read continued to increase in bounding strides until the letters formed a tendril-like mass upon the page and he felt himself become entangled within the curly flourishes. Instead of reading, he began watching the boy in the meadow struggling to run through long grasses which became longer and denser and blacker against the blue tone of the page on which the scene played out. With a sharp inhalation, he tore his eyes from the page and stared out of the window as he tried to regulate his breathing. He felt sick. He lay the tips of his fingers on Inspector Bell's letter and turned back to look at it. The text lay still on the page; an elegant account of an educated man. Above his fingertips about three quarters of the way down the page he read "in the depths of the wood, near to Cadbury Castle, we located the cave presumably that referred to in the letter". Hingston slid his fingers to the bottom of the page. "Indeed, the cave had been recently inhabited and dried holly branches were found of a similar size to that Miss Tolcher had placed on the ground where Charles Embling had met his death."

Hingston shook his head as he continued to read. "On a ledge, halfway into the cave we discovered a knife, stained with what appeared to be blood. The knife blade is some eight inches in length and appears sharp enough to have caused the effect of almost decapitating the boy."

Hingston visualised the way the police may have approached the bloody weapon; staring at it in dim lamplight, resting upon the ledge and casting a jet black shadow against the stone. He imagined their eyes darting up and down its length, noting the dried, sorrowful streaks of haemoglobin which with its brown hue sinisterly mimicked the common form of a rusted iron blade. He sensed the dank December drizzle and the slippery chill inside the cave which would have emanated from the rocks and passed into the lifeless wooden handle of the knife. He longed for the ability to reach out and take that knife before the Victorian police swooped upon it with a pocket handkerchief. He yearned to rescue that significant piece of evidence and whisk it away in a secure plastic bag to the forensics laboratory.

He read on, continuing overleaf. "We proceeded to the abode of Miss Tolcher whereupon we entered by her invitation. Spurred presumably by the seriousness of our tone and what I presume to be her own guilt, Miss Tolcher produced a pocket watch and made claim that an intruder had entered her home last night and deposited it. She stated she had witnessed a man run out of her lodgings and down the lane, but could only describe him as tall with whiskers. She appeared troubled and stated she had not before seen the watch, neither had she any knowledge of the owner or why it would have been placed by the fire in her lodgings. The watch was clearly of value which would be significant compared to Miss Tolcher's earnings as a weaver. Upon inspection of the watch, I observed the initials R.J.E."

Hingston caught his breath and began to splutter, drawing a look of disapproval from a silver-haired gentleman who was reading at the next table. He regained his position within Inspector Bell's letter. "Surmising these initials to be those of Mr Richard Embling, I informed Miss Tolcher that we had attended her address having discovered a bloodied knife in a cave near Cadbury Castle which we had reason to believe she occupied and for that reason I would be arresting her on suspicion of committing the murder of Charles Embling." Hingston felt his cheeks start to burn. "The woman cried inconsolably."

Why would Miss Tolcher reveal the pocket watch if she was the murderer, Hingston questioned himself. If she did so to divert suspicion to the mystery intruder who was "tall with whiskers", what made her take the risk of fabricating a story? How would she have known the police had discovered the knife? *Did* she know the police had discovered the knife? Was she actually telling them the truth? Was there, in reality, a mystery intruder? Again, Hingston skimmed through the paperwork for some answers, noting key words and passages he would return to later.

Without warning, he felt a tightening in his chest and his mouth began to dry. He blinked repeatedly and turned onto a page of statements at which point his forehead went into spasm between his eyebrows; the twisting sensation vibrated inside his head like the musical box being cranked up with its winding key. Forced to shut his eyes, Hingston hoped the pain would stop. The twisting continued for two more turns and released like a tightly wound spring. A torrent of colours flashed behind his eyelids, red, blue and silver. They passed hypnotically and as the pain vaporised and his forehead relaxed, a series of images began to intersperse between the colours.

The images were fuzzy at first, little more than grainy splodges of colour like those seen on waking from a deep sleep. As the images sharpened, Hingston could make out three separate scenes; a paddock of horses, a brook and a girl. With his eyes closed he continued to watch in a surreal, dream inspired state. The horses were white, silver and brown and were many in number. The brook sparkled and the girl intrigued him. As each image of the girl darted before his eyes, her face became closer and clearer. She was beautiful to Hingston and young. Her hair was blonde and pinned back softly from her face which was decorated with makeup, especially her lips. Her lips were scarlet and shone dramatically against her porcelain features. He stared at those lips as the three flashing colours reduced down to red; the girl's face, red, the girl's face, red, the girl's lips, red, the girl's strawberry shaped lips, red, the girl's scarlet lips parted, red, the girl's face contorted and *screaming*; screaming which rang in Hingston's ears as if she were stood directly behind his head. He forced his eyes open and gasped for air. All was silent in the reading room. His right hand was pressed down across the delicate blue pages. Staring back at him from the line which ran from the nail of his little finger to his wrist were the inked words "maintains it was the man, tall with whiskers". His ears continued to resonate from the scream.

Chapter Ten
What a Performance

Dazzling white spots of sunlight decorated dark green glossy leaves. Gigantic palms with furry brown trunks towered above shiny shrubbery to cast a dappled shade upon them. Peeping out between the heights of the backlit canopy and the dense tropical carpet were fancy flowers of hot pink, salsa red and Brazilian orange which posed provocatively like Latino ladies looking for love. A sweet steaminess exuded from every pocket of this hot energy hub and settled on Hingston's skin. There was something invigorating yet relaxing about the glass houses at Kew Gardens which made Hingston desire a visit; he considered it to be a holistic approach to dealing with his unsettling morning at The National Archives.

Before he left the Archives he photocopied every page of the Castle Wood murder file so that he could continue to read and digest its contents at home. He decided this was the most effective way to absorb the facts of the investigation or indeed be absorbed by the investigation, whichever of the two was going to occur. Furthermore, he would not have to put up with the filthy looks cast at him by the silver-haired gentleman or, for that matter, the other readers who had become irritated after he gasped upon seeing and hearing the screaming girl.

Hingston's phone began to vibrate: incoming call, Fynn Mannix.

'Fynn!' answered Hingston. He had not spoken with Mannix since the incident at the City of London Police Museum.

'Jason! How are you doing?'

'Yeah, I'm fine,' Hingston bluffed. 'Just strolling round Kew Gardens.'

'Nice day for it, Jason. Look, I've heard they've signed you off and I wanted you to know that if there's anything I can do, just give me a shout. I've worked Missing Persons in my time. I understand the stresses and strains,' Mannix offered.

'Thanks, Fynn. I've had a week down in Dartmouth. First day back in London.'

'Getting time to take your mind off things, then?'

'Well,' Hingston did not want to lie to his friend. 'I'm definitely looking at things from a different perspective. Trying to turn the negatives into positives. Think the break's working!' He laughed to try to reassure Mannix that everything was okay.

'That's sounding good, Jason. Changing the subject, you know that historian you stood up? She was a bit of a looker!'

'Oh, really! You trying to rub it in now?' Hingston laughed.

'The other guys were pleased you weren't there. They wouldn't have had a chance otherwise!' Mannix was a practiced leg-puller.

'Yeah, I believe you!' said Hingston. 'You'll have to invite her back again, for me!'

'If I do, it'll be for me!' Mannix chuckled.

The signal began to break up.

'Fynn. I'll get back in touch with you in a few weeks. Thanks for your support.'

'Anytime,' said Mannix.

Hingston breathed in the moist air, just as one treating stubborn congestion would inhale steam rising from a bowl with great determination to recover. The images he saw at The National Archives remained with him during his walk through the luscious vegetation, as did the sound of the musical box chimes which soothed him and allowed him to refocus in time for his drive home.

* * *

The copies of Inspector Bell's file sat on the leather of Hingston's desk as he lay down on his bed and closed his eyes in thought. The musical box sat silently by his side on top of the duvet and the May sunshine lit the room through the open window. A cooling breeze drifted into Hingston's bedroom, brushing his cheek. A gentle calm soothed him into a peaceful sleep. And then, when his overworked mind relaxed, he reached a pivotal moment; a moment which grasped him by the heart and dragged him into a world which sparkled in shades of blue, silver and red.

A very small hole was the viewing point through which shiny coated, muscular horses could be seen prancing and galloping around a ring, kicking up golden sawdust against a colourful backdrop. Riding on the backs of the horses were women performing dangerous acrobatic manoeuvres. They called to each other periodically whilst rehearsing this spectacular routine which clearly required the greatest skills of a tested choreographer to ensure a catastrophic accident could most likely be avoided. The routine ended and without break began once again.

Hingston's view of the scene expanded as if he were now positioned close to the performance. A short, rotund man of at least fifty years stood outside the ring drinking from a dark coloured jug. His russet red face was well worn and as he shouted instructions to the women from his thick, chapped lips, his drink sprayed out in tiny droplets from the gaps between his partially rotted, yellow-brown teeth.

In walked another man; taller with a sallow appearance, and he leered at the women. His dark eyes moved manically as he followed the firm, curvaceous limbs and corseted busts around the ring.

The horses' hooves thudded, their nostrils flared and snorted and their tails flowed and flicked as they wove in and out of each other.

The sallow man chewed on tobacco and with an unnecessary display of teeth and tongue he passed crass comments and gestured perversely to the rotund man who laughed with him occasionally in an equally chauvinistic manner.

The routine ended once more and jumping from her horse, one of the women came bounding over to the men. Familiar with them both, she took a sip of whatever alcohol remained in the jug held by the rotund man, undeterred by the mix of drink and saliva which shone around his crusty lips. She then winked at him and squeezed the crutch of the taller man. He lifted her up, dangled her over his shoulder and paraded her out of the tent, laughing, her short dress failing to hide her vibrant undergarments.

The remaining women stretched and chatted by the horses, accustomed to the habits of the men.

Outside the lit tent the surroundings were cold and dark. Two further tents were pitched up in the near vicinity and into the smallest, the equestrienne and the taller man entered.

The scene was loud with colour. A heap of spangled costumes lay strewn over bales of hay. Props, wigs and tools littered the area. Amongst the mayhem, a raucous crowd of males fell around on their seats as beer was shared and shabby cards, dirty coins and ragged notes were grasped, slammed on the makeshift table and snatched back and forth between them.

The equestrienne kicked her muscular legs playfully as she was carried between the gamblers. She was laughing and shouting profanity at the back of her testosterone-charged, swarthy punter.

Only the attention of a boot button eyed marmoset wearing a shiny red waistcoat was caught as the pair strode by. The marmoset cocked his head and his gleaming, round eyes sparkled before he jumped up and down on the card table making strange noises like a cat on helium.

A boss-eyed gambler gave an almighty cheer and in a display of bigoted camaraderie, the tall, sallow man grappled with the equestrienne's blue satin undergarments. He performed a jubilatory double turn which gave rise to two cacophonic salutations from his grubby audience, following which he walked his bare-bottomed trophy behind a heavy piece of canvas.

The gamblers were a mismatched set; some in their twenties and thirties, others a generation older and whether they were from Britain or beyond, it was impossible to tell for they spoke over each other incessantly and cheered, groaned and complained throughout the fast-paced card game. There was the boss-eyed fellow who may or may not have been biologically advantaged for cheating; there was a tiny man of only three foot six; a lanky specimen with gangly arms and legs; a pair of large, muscular men who flexed their biceps and visibly tightened their neck muscles when the game was not going their way; a balding, stout, pasty individual with a rasping cough; a long haired wizard-like character who laughed incredibly deeply for his tiny frame and a bearded red-head who was chunky, of tall stature and morose.

Moments later, in poured a number of the other equestriennes, some of whom flocked to the gamblers, giggling and flirting with them all, even with the most unlikely of the unattractive collection.

The bearded red-head rose from his seat and grabbed the tiny waist of a dark haired equestrienne who was wearing emerald green and red. Unimpressed by his groping attentions, she slapped him about his face and returned to giggling with the stout individual with the rasping cough.

The stout man had a distinctive presence; his age, stodgy cheeks, fat stomach and his well-tailored trousers and jacket suggested he had money. Furthermore, he did not even need to glare at the red-head; it took only a look to mark his territory and make the miserable monstrosity skulk away.

On his way out of the tent, the red-head grabbed a mallet and tossed it back and forth between his giant sized hands and this created a sharp slapping sound which reverberated in the chill of the night. He turned around violently and hurled the mallet into the darkness. As he clenched his teeth and growled, the moisture from his cavernous lungs poured out of his nostrils and escaped from between his beer drenched teeth and receding gums. He proceeded into the ring where the women had been rehearsing. The short, rotund man was still interlocking his lips with his jug which had been refilled since earlier. The high wire loomed overhead, unused and still. The horses had been removed and tethered somewhere away from the ring and acrobats and jugglers practiced complicated routines in their place. Enraged by the absence of any females, the seething red-head stamped his way through the sawdust and headed toward the third tent.

The third tent was unlit and quiet. Several carriage trunks were stacked up and others were scattered about higgledy-piggledy. The cold of the night had infiltrated this tent and it felt lifeless. As the red-head stepped on the crunchy sawdust he heard a voice whisper then stop abruptly. He noticed a faint glow beyond the trunks and reached toward a long, black leather whip.

'Crrraackk!' The whip slapped upon the nearest trunk and the tent filled with noise instantaneously. Growls and hisses and hoots and squawks amalgamated into a horrendous chorus of panic. The beating of wings and the whooshing of tails sounded hard against the iron bars which caged the menagerie. In the dim light, the occasional glimmer of wild eyes could be seen glaring out of the trunks.

The faint glow was extinguished post-haste.

The red-head strode between the trunks and detected the sweet aroma of candle wax and smoke.

The menagerie's furore began to calm just before there was a sudden rush of footfalls in the sawdust.

The insane red-head bellowed in what could only be described as a war cry and lashed out with his whip, striking the delicate wrist of a young girl. Her cry of pain was lost to the second burst of wild hysteria which sounded from the trunks and the red-head lunged towards her. She was carried from the tent under his right arm and her teenage legs kicked out in fear with as much effect on him as a captured frog would have on the claws of a red shouldered hawk.

He marched her into the frosty outdoors where a black velvet sky offset a shiny silver moon. Swathes of stars were suspended above and they had the same appearance as magician's glitter blown from a clenched fist a thousand times over. The metallic light shone down upon her and embellished her soft blonde hair and her scarlet lips. Her helpless eyes stared ahead. A solitary sparkling tear quivered on her porcelain cheek like a liquid diamond which reflected the light of the silver stars above. And as that tear fell into the darkness everything went black.

Fighting for air as if he had just resurfaced from a capsized boat, Hingston threw himself upright on his bed. His heart was thumping to the point his eardrums were pulsating and his throat felt swollen. He exhaled through his mouth and his chest shook on each inhalation. Hingston placed his hands above his temples and poked his fingers into his hair which was damp and tacky from the mix of styling wax and perspiration. The bedroom was unchanged from earlier, but he felt different. The sun and the breeze entered through his window and he wiped the sweat from his top lip on the back of his hand. Oblivious to how much time had passed, he could remember every minute detail of the scenes that had unfolded before him. As he pursed his lips in contemplation, thinking about the girl with the scarlet lips, the girl whose face had made a lasting impression upon him at the Archives this morning and again just now, he turned to the musical box beside him on the duvet.

With a gentle turn of the key, he opened up the golden world of pins and headed not for the winding key, but for the wad of newspaper. Folded as neatly as when he first found it, the compact beige paper felt warm and intriguing. There, on the reverse side to the dentistry advert, he reread the glorious grey letters:

KALLENSEE'S GREAT CIRCUS
WILL VISIT EXETER ON WEDNESDAY, 17 OCTOBER
AND GIVE TWO GRAND REPRESENTATIONS
AFTERNOON OPEN AT 2.15, COMMENCING AT 2.45.
EVENING OPEN AT 7.15, COMMENCING AT 7.45.
Equestrian Wonders – Matchless Clowns – Wire Walkers –
Contortionists –Acrobatic Artistes – Feats of Juggling – Menagerie
and other attractions.

The acts exploded into life. The taste of sawdust filled his mouth with a new significance and the face of the girl with the scarlet lips prevailed in his mind.

Hingston rose to his feet, for this was significant. He ran down the staircase, wad of newspaper in his left hand, his right skimming the banister and entered his study. His imposing desk was before him with an investigation file on it and in his hand was a piece of evidence which had been locked inside a murdered boy's musical box for almost one hundred and fifty years.

Chapter Eleven
A New Dawn

The grandfather clock chimed twice when Hingston reached the last page of the murder file. The night had been long. As a result, Hingston's eyes were sore and bloodshot from his prolonged reading of the photocopied Victorian handwriting.

His desk was covered with neat piles of papers which he had grouped into categories, highlighted in yellow and referenced onto a pad of paper which displayed his observations, deductions and questions. He finally felt the elderly woman's advice about the ebb and flow of the sea was correct. The answers he sought were beginning to surface like pebbles returning to a beach.

He sighed as he leaned back in his chair. It was at this desk he studied for his national policing examinations. He was very fond of the gilt tooled moss green leather top which was offset by the rich red tones of the mahogany. Sitting at this chunky antique desk with its nine drawers and solid plinth base made him feel focused.

The piece of newspaper which bragged about Kallensee's Circus sat central in the back row of papers and Hingston stared at it angrily. Mr Kallensee, Mr Bibbings and Mr Crim, the Circus' Proprietor, Acting Manager and Clown, had taken on a dark, grimy persona which Hingston had welded to his memory of the garish, sordid and deplorable scenes. He read their names with a frown upon his pink forehead which had been fingered and rubbed over the past eight and three quarter hours. He severed his chain of thought, rose to his feet and headed for the kitchen.

Pack of biscuits in hand, he flopped into his beloved leather sofa and turned on the news. He blinked and held the biscuits still as he saw the blue backdrop with the words Metropolitan Police stamped on it. In the fore were the two distraught faces of Mr and Mrs Clarke. They were glancing up from their laps periodically and Hingston watched the reddened, shaking hand of Mrs Clarke dart to her eyes with a screwed up tissue every few seconds. The press appeal was a repeat from an early evening release which Hingston had missed whilst researching the Emblings.

'…whoever is holding Nathan, wherever he is, we want to have him back home…' Mrs Clarke, overcome with emotion, stifled her heavy sobbing into her tissue and her shoulders jerked. The press photographers' cameras flashed and clattered.

A teary eyed Mr Clarke took over from his wife, having tightened his grip around her back and squeezed her towards him to plant an empty kiss upon her head. 'Nathan, if you're watching this, I want you to know it will all be okay… we're not going to give up looking for you. Your mum, your brother Robert, your sister Alice and me need you back home… we love you…' Mr Clarke blurted the last words before he and his wife looked into each other's eyes and showed the world they had virtually given up hope. The death of Daniel and the absence of any arrest had shattered them.

Hingston tossed the pack of biscuits onto the coffee table next to his untouched cup of tea. He massaged his eyebrows and ran his hands over his eyes and down his cheeks. He recalled the statements of Richard and Elizabeth Embling; two devastated parents who had no explanation to offer as to the disappearance of their twin boys; two devoted parents who just like the Clarkes wanted nothing more than to find the surviving twin. But George Embling was never found. How could Nathan Clarke be found?

Hingston shook his head and visualised the papers in his study. There was no rational explanation or logical reason he could think of to prevent himself from being perceived as a desperate officer losing his grip on his remaining scraps of sanity. But it had to be done. He walked back into his study. On one stack of paper a sentence glowed vibrantly: "I hasten to report that John Embling, one of the younger brothers of Charles and George, has this morning been reported missing from the family residence".

Hingston strummed his fingers on his desk as he stood looking down at this sentence. John Embling, like George Embling, had no death certificate; he was also never found. As far as was recorded within Inspector Bell's investigation, it was concluded that John Embling had fled the family home ten days after the discovery of Charles' body due to the trauma he had experienced. John had taken his overcoat and had stolen two £1 notes before his departure, but there was no trace of him. An eight-year-old boy heading off into the December chill, even with an overcoat and a significant amount of money, could easily have met his death within forty-eight hours.

Hingston had earlier pinpointed Newton St Cyres on a map of Devon and calculated its distance from nearby parishes and to Cadbury where Charles Embling's body was discovered. Newton St Cyres was a small dot amongst miles of open countryside and had John headed for Cadbury, the journey would have been around six miles; provided he succeeded in taking a direct route without losing his bearings amongst the fields.

Hingston tried to think back to when he was an eight-year-old in an attempt to fathom out a young boy's logic. He wanted to believe that there was a purpose to John's disappearance and therefore discarded the notion that he had run away traumatised. He felt Inspector Bell was wrong and had credited John with little intelligence. Surely, an upset eight-year-old would want the comfort of his parents; the sense of security that he would surely feel within his own home and with his own belongings? To steal two £1 notes suggested he had formulated a plan and intended to fend for himself for some time. This left Hingston with two possible reasons for John Embling's departure: to visit the site of Charles' murder or to find George. Whichever of the two applied, John Embling had *planned* to leave and if it were to find George, then John knew something he failed to share with any of his family, let alone the police.

Hingston continued to stare at the sentence of Inspector Bell's report then looked at his watch. In the morning he would contact the murder squad and advise them to approach the Clarkes to gain access to Robert. If the Embling twins' brother knew something of their whereabouts then Hingston believed the chances were, the same would apply now.

Hingston's eyes skimmed over the piles of paper which were illuminated by his sturdy brass desk lamp. Nearest the lamp was the paperwork relating to the mystery intruder: "tall with whiskers". He gave a sigh which conveyed both irritation and deflatedness. His mind filled with the assurances of Inspector Bell that thorough enquiries revealed no such individual and that no witnesses came forward to corroborate the account of Miss Tolcher, but Hingston felt a heavy weight in his chest. The weight was like a giant chunk of seaside rock and through it ran the words "tall with whiskers".

It had been confirmed by Mr and Mrs Embling that the silver pocket watch engraved with the letters R.J.E. did belong to Mr Embling and that he had not noticed its absence until the police had returned it. It was one of his personal items that sat within a drawer of a cabinet and was infrequently used. Hingston continued to mull over Miss Tolcher's surrender of the pocket watch and her robust maintenance of her account which remained unchanged up to and including the 6th of May 1867; the day she was hanged at Devon County Gaol.

He yawned and his sore eyes were bathed in warm tears which moistened his lower lashes. It was time to call it a night. Hingston placed his middle finger on the switch of his desk lamp and extinguished the light. The whole room went black and the glow from the hallway was lost.

'Bloody power cut!' Hingston grumbled. His finger had remained on the switch and in frustration he pressed it again. All the lights returned. Hingston looked about his study with a perplexed expression. He walked into the hall and could hear the television playing to itself in the lounge.

The perplexed expression had not faded when he returned to his desk and replaced his finger on the switch. With mild hesitation he depressed it and watched his paperwork lose its light like embers which puff their last glow into the darkness. The hallway light remained on and he could hear the advertisements being aired on the television a noticeable few decibels louder than the news.

He raised his eyebrows, puckered his bottom lip and headed for the door.

'Cluuunkk.' The power was lost again.

'What the…' Hingston groaned. The room was pitch black and he felt for the gloss painted doorway. There was no reason to expect the power to return any time soon. As he stepped into the hallway the blackness felt richer and there was a sweetness in the air. He looked in the direction of the lounge and saw a faint shimmer of light which he approached suspiciously. Hingston poked his head around the door and was confronted with a cold gust of air. He gasped with fear of both the unknown and for his sanity. The lounge had become an open expanse and he raised his eyes to behold a midnight sky of silver stars. Panicked and confused, Hingston fumbled for the familiar feel of the doorway whilst his eyes remained fixed upon the stars. He could not reach it, so squeezed his eyes closed and spun around to face the hall. Upon opening them, he found a moonlit field and he knew where he was instantly.

Hingston began to turn on the spot and observed his breath float into the frosty night air and dissipate. He continued to turn, overwhelmed and feeling lost. In the blink of an eye three familiar tents appeared before him and he felt a bitter taste of anger pass down his throat. He walked towards the tents, his senses heightened and his heart racing. As he approached the darkened tent he could hear the wild bewailing blast behind the canvas. With the same sensation Hingston imagined would be experienced if one could step into a well-watched film, he neared the entrance to the tent and waited.

The canvas cracked and out thundered the red-head with his prey clasped under his arm. Hingston watched her legs thrash out defencelessly as she was carried into the night. Allowing a few seconds' gap, he followed in pursuit, his bare feet feeling chilled by the moist grass. A piercing pain passed through his head like a knitting needle inserted, twisted and aggressively removed. The spasm forced his eyes to close and when he opened them the beautiful girl with the blonde pinned back hair and the shiny scarlet lips was lying clumsily and tense upon heaps of vulgar fabric coloured blue, silver and red. Her eyes were shimmering with moisture and her chest was rising and falling rapidly with fear. She wriggled backwards and kicked out with her legs, but the dense fabric cushioned and enveloped her like chunky tendrils of ivy restraining a delicate rose.

Hingston's eyes were fixed on the scene. His body and his vocal chords were rigid and cold. A dark silhouette appeared in his line of view. It was the red-head towering above the girl and he came close to her and removed his belt roughly, grunting in temper as he yanked it from his trousers. His aggression filled the air like one hundred foul smelling joss sticks lit inside a broom cupboard.

The girl brought her arms up over her chest and shielded her face with her hands. A deep red-purple double bracelet glowed from her wrist which Hingston knew had been created by the red-head's whip.

The veins on the male's arm pulsated as he increased his grip on the belt and in a manner as if he was beating a rabid ferret he struck the girl with the buckle of the belt three times then stopped.

She remained silent and he remained silent. All that could be heard was her shuddering high pitched breaths and his hollow exhalations as he stood upright and glared at her down his raised, sneering nose. Her arms remained squeezed around herself and blood ran from her brow and her cheek where the metal had hammered against her porcelain skin.

Suddenly, her eyes averted from the mountainous miscreation and with an outstretched, shaking arm she looked into Hingston's soul and screamed.

The red-head threw back his shoulders and turned to the right; the girl's scream continued to sound and the light bounced off his beard like brilliant red flames. His eyes interlocked with Hingston's and his heavy frowning brow met his snarling nose.

Hingston bellowed and his countertenor note harmonised with the girl's piercing soprano in a full throttle cry befitting a tragic opera.

Instantaneously all went black as if the curtain had prematurely fallen upon the scene. All that remained was Hingston's wailing. Sweating and shaking he thrust himself about and then it became apparent to him that he was on his bed.

The grandfather clock chimed five. Sunrise. Panting and confused, he reached for the musical box. Its cheerful melody sang out and he fingered the small brass key with a renewed sense of awe and respect.

Chapter Twelve
Prioritise, Prioritise, Prioritise

As a DS, Hingston knew only too well the pressures of modern day policing. Amongst the caseloads, the managerial responsibilities, the challenging shift patterns with the need for overtime but the financial requirement to cut back on overtime, the organisational changes and the public scrutiny, was the constant demand for performance improvement. Sometimes it felt no more than a game of numbers; a ranking system blown out of proportion and out of control. However, it had taught him how to prioritise. The Clarke twins' case would be one of the key priorities at present and gaining access to Robert Clarke should be the key priority within it, not that the murder squad may realise that as yet.

Hingston headed to Hounslow Police Station straight after a five thirty breakfast, his aim to speak with the Senior Investigating Officer at the start of the early turn shift. He parked at the front of the drab, box shaped, brick building, directly in line with the brilliant blue police lamp. He stared at the lamp and considered it to be the only remaining traditional symbol that the large, ugly police station had to offer.

As he lost himself in thought, gazing into the Prussian blue glass, he was reminded of Brace's dismissal of his telephone call to her. Not only did she refuse to take his call seriously, she stated she would advise Occupational Health that he was still troubled by the case. He had not been contacted by Occupational Health as a result, but then why would they do that? He had a check-up appointment in a little short of two weeks. More questions knocked on the door to his mind with the persistence of unwanted salesmen. When he speaks with the Senior Investigating Officer, will he receive the same dismissive response from him? Will the SIO know that he is signed off and technically not supposed to be at the station, let alone attempting to get involved with the case? The nagging questions spun around his brain. Hingston grabbed the car door handle and stepped out onto the sunny tarmac. He adjusted his tie and checked his warrant card was displayed on his trouser belt.

Confidently, he walked to the station reception and swiped into the main building. He was familiar with the layout of the offices and navigated himself up the blue tiled staircases and the blue-grey corridors until he arrived at the rear of the building on the second floor.

A pungent, musky aftershave permeated the corridor, its origin the bald, muscular SIO named Detective Chief Inspector Smythe. His office was pokey and lit dimly, worsened by a sizeable wardrobe which contained his many uniforms and displayed a horde of football trophies on the top of it. The cupboard was open and DCI Smythe was inspecting himself in the mirror on the inside of the door.

Hingston smiled to himself as he observed Smythe straighten his suit jacket before inflating his chest, placing his hands in his trouser pockets, re-straightening his jacket and performing an Elvis lip sideways on in the mirror.

Hingston paused before knocking on the office door.

'DS Jason Hing—ston! Good morning to you,' Smythe boomed in his husky voice and gave an intense stare with his dark eyes.

'Morning, sir,' Hingston replied with a mild smile and noticed the DCI's once bushy eyebrows had been clipped into shape and his clean shaven face glowed with an unnatural tan.

'You must be here about the Clarkes, otherwise you'd be, er, where is it? Chiswick. Yes, posh old Chiswick,' he snorted in a "posh old" accent applied for satirical effect.

Hingston didn't warm to his humour or his arrogance, but replied politely. Apparently, the DCI did not know he was signed off which pleased Hingston.

'D'you mind if we talk this way?' Smythe gestured with his hand out of the room. 'I need to get some toast before I fade away.' He clasped his hands and rubbed them together. His biceps pressed against his jacket sleeves and his solid chest filled his shirt which should have been a collar size bigger.

'I want to address a matter concerning Robert Clarke, sir.' Hingston launched into the purpose of his visit a few doors down the corridor in the kitchen.

'Fire away,' Smythe commanded as he loaded four slices of bread into the toaster.

'The statement of Robert Clarke focuses on the events of April fifteenth and how that differed from the boys' normal routine. What we haven't explored is Robert's understanding of his brothers; what they are like, how they interact with each other, with him, at home. Yes, we've got the parents' and school teachers' perspectives, but Robert may be the key to finding out more.'

'Then why didn't you pursue this, DS Hingston?' the DCI challenged as he banged the marmite jar on the counter and opened the cutlery drawer noisily.

'I sought this evidence, but the Clarkes refused access to Robert,' Hingston responded. 'They insisted they'd discussed everything openly and fully as a family and had nothing more to give us.'

Smythe rummaged in the drawer for a reasonably clean knife. 'And you're pressing for this now and not *before* Daniel's murder *i.e.* in the four-five weeks in which he was still alive, *because*?'

'Because we're dealing with a murder now; the parents may now be persuaded and…' Hingston paused to consider his words. 'The more I've considered Robert Clarke's statement, the more controlled and simplistic it feels. I think he may know or suspect something he was purposefully holding back on.' Hingston knew he had to keep the Emblings' case out of it.

'Firstly, DS Hingston, you're wrong,' Smythe blasted. '*We're* not dealing with a murder, *I* am and *my* team are. Secondly, you're signed off so I don't know what you're doing on police premises and thirdly, if you've got a suggestion to share,' he cleared his throat and stepped nearer to Hingston, 'call me on my fucking mobile.' He pulled a business card from his top pocket and handed it to Hingston.

'Okay, sir,' he confirmed with a slight nod.

'I don't know why they signed you off. You're a good detective and you seem perfectly all right to me,' the DCI remarked. His bread sprung out of the toaster with a loud ping. 'I'll see what we can achieve with the Clarkes.'

Hingston returned to his car with his satisfaction thermometer glowing brightly. He mentally checked off Robert Clarke from his list and headed back to Hatch End with an energised optimism.

* * *

Hingston lay on his sofa with his eyes closed for a good half hour whilst he collected his thoughts. The undoubted parallels between the Clarkes and the Emblings set him cross-referencing the cases.

Hingston already suspected the Clarke twins planned to run away and orchestrated their disappearance so as to leave no social footprint on or offline. The Embling twins apparently also left no trace, but Hingston suspected they had hidden away one clue now discovered, the newspaper cutting advertising Kallensee's Great

Circus. In those days, wasn't it many young boys' dream to run away to the circus? Why else have the cutting inside the musical box? Why else would he be experiencing such life-like dreams or visions which have coincided with his review of the Embling murder file? The connection between the Clarkes and the Emblings was too significant to be coincidental.

Last night, as part of his reinvestigation, he accessed the online newspaper archive and searched for Kallensee's Circus. From 1865 to 1868 they toured England. They clearly didn't advertise every performance in the newspaper, only those at major towns and the first and last of the season. The last of the 1866 season, as in 1865, was in Silverton, a village around seven miles from Exeter and five from Cadbury. Over winter they would have set up their tents and portable lodgings to rehearse for the coming season's performances. Maybe they were pitched up near to Cadbury and near to Castle Wood where Charles Embling's body was found? But if so, how were they missed from the investigation conducted by Inspector Bell? What is the significance of the girl with the red lips and porcelain features? Who was she? Is it too much to query whether the monstrous, bearded red-head could actually be the male described by Miss Tolcher as "tall with whiskers"?

The multitude of unanswered questions mingled and merged together as they jostled for space in Hingston's overcrowded mind. His subconscious kicked into action and behind his darkened eyelids he imagined the motion of the River Dart. On each tiny wave his questions fell into an order and bobbed alongside each other. He breathed in a meditative state. A seagull swooped into the scene and caught his attention, for his visit to Dartmouth had given him a distinct disliking of these birds. As he focused on the seagull a whisper, no louder than the wind lifting the gull's wings, breathed 'it is not always possible to *understand…*' and Hingston opened his eyes.

Involuntarily, he was using the advice of the elderly woman. The waves, the ebb and flow of the sea and the opening of his mind was the technique shared by her. The whispered words were hers. And then he remembered. The past week had been so chaotic it was not really any surprise he had forgotten. The evening of the fish and chips, when the elderly woman told him it's not always possible to understand, it was *that* evening she scolded him when he joked about the absence of crime in Devon. She also said something about felony.

'What was it? What was it?' Hingston muttered. He tried to think back to the evening and to his pebble skimming at Blackpool Sands, anything which may assist in recalling her words. It was to no avail. However, he was soon formulating a new train of thought based on the old woman's reference to felony and that she clearly held a passionate view on the subject.

As Hingston had expressed to Uncle Zack, he was suspicious of her apparent ability to judge him and possibly even read his thoughts. However, if she were reliant on some form of mind reading technique, then she most definitely was not using it at the juncture where felony was raised; at that time Hingston was oblivious to the case of the Embling twins and Daniel Clarke had not been murdered.

Hingston's nostrils flared and he felt a prickliness around his neck. Had she predicted what was going to happen? The elderly woman's insightful comments were taking on a new significance. Was she, like a rudder to his boat, steering him through this mind-warping wormhole to the past? A past which has attached itself to the present like nucleotides which join to form the double helical structure of DNA? Was this representative of the Emblings and the Clarkes; two sets of twins, two twinned murders? New questions began to form. *Who is* the elderly woman? *What* does she know? *How* does she know? *Why* is she interested? She said that when stood under the saffron street light she was there as "a reminder". Hingston could not forget the curly haired boy who was present seconds before her under the same light. A connection between the two could not be ignored.

Hingston's pupils dilated and his brown eyes sparkled. The boy in the meadow *must* be one of the Embling twins! His chest rose and his eyes stared like well-polished saucers. The braces, the hairstyle, the open expanse through which the boy was running; the boy's perpetual appearance since the night terrors began and the meadow itself, its brilliant image upon the golden grain of the musical box when he found it in Totnes. The clues had been there all along, but his mind was not open to the depths of this illogical possibility until now: he finally accepted that it is *not* always possible to understand.

* * *

Hingston strummed his fingers on his steering wheel and checked and rechecked his rear-view mirror. Wednesday night was overcast and wet. By ten thirty it was torrential and the mechanics of his wipers whined and groaned like a bored child who suffered from car sickness. He was outside Hounslow Police Station under the blue lamp which was now luminous against the dreary night sky.

His eyes flicked up to his rear-view mirror and he finally caught sight of a darkened, hunched figure. The passenger door flew open and the soggy, steamy individual dropped into the seat and slammed the door. Droplets of rain sprinkled upon the dash, the handbrake and Hingston's trousers. The fragrant, moist heap passed no comment on the foul weather.

Hingston turned the ignition. 'KFC?'

'McDonald's,' was the immediate reply.

'Bath Road then,' Hingston decided. 'Thanks for seeing me tonight,' he added and glanced past his passenger to reverse through the torrent. Manoeuvre executed, he smiled expectantly at his dinner date.

'Jason! I've been at it for ten and a half hours,' she blinked her pale green eyes dramatically. 'Can we just get the food first!' The blinking of the eyes was like her trademark. Regardless of the hairstyle changes and the image reinvention when she moved from uniform to become a DC, Remi's eyes were always her iconic, dazzling characteristic.

'Okay,' Hingston laughed and tried to push back memories of the past. 'I can wait.'

'Are you being sarcastic or are you just as impatient as ever!' She rested her elbow on the plastic facade of the car door and with a flick of her wrist gestured with her open palm and widespread fingers.

Hingston grinned and laughed silently to himself as he threw the car into first gear and up to second to make a swooping exit from the police station. He felt as though the two years since their relationship ended had just evaporated, for Remi seemed to be as bold and vivacious as she was when *he* was a new DC and she was patrolling Chiswick in uniform; young, ambitious and energetic. 'Enjoying the life of a DC?' Hingston quizzed as a matter of small talk because he knew her response.

'It's fantastic. Best move. Definitely best move so far,' she nodded.

Their conversation had barely begun when they reached the Drive Thru. Hingston placed the order through the intercom and the rain pounded off the top of its silver coloured surround. He drove round to the first window to join the queue.

'I'm not starting until I've eaten half of that burger,' Remi stated to Hingston and smiled, her immaculate teeth being concealed behind her rosebud pink lips.

'Okay!' Hingston stressed. 'We'll talk about something else… okay,' he smiled. 'What would you have been doing if I hadn't called in a favour and treated you to a Maccy-D's?'

Remi looked into his eyes and blinked once whilst she considered her reply. 'Ooh… traffic's moving,' she pointed out.

Hingston moved further up behind the Renault, aware he may have asked an awkward question. Did it sound like he was prying? Chatting her up? He swallowed self-consciously. Perhaps he was? 'Only a few more feet and we'll be getting those burgers.' He decided to take the pressure off.

'Ordinarily I would have been going round to Rob's,' she advised in a matter of fact tone and stared at the brake lights of the Renault.

Hingston also stared at the brake lights as he digested her comment.

There were a lot of Robs in the force and their mug shots filled his mind with feelings of envy, surprise, bewilderment and in one or two instances, revulsion. One that stood out was that of *his* DC. 'Not DC Rob *Barker*?' he pried without shame. He glanced at her face which was lit by the red glow of the brake light. As he stared ahead he felt his cheeks heat up to match the burning colour. He felt let down by his DC. *Everyone* knew he had been in a long term relationship with Remi. Surely, common decency on the part of Rob…

'Smythe,' she stated in an irritated tone which told Hingston he should not have continued his prying.

Hingston looked at her aghast. 'What are you doing with that tosser?'

Remi glared at him and had turned round in her seat so as to hurl back her response. 'That *tosser* is your superior, Jason. Have you no respect?'

'A few pips on the shoulder mean nothing. *Well*, it obviously means a lot to his over inflated ego… the puffed up, poncy…'

He was interrupted by an angry '*Beeeeeeeep!*' from the car behind him.

Hingston lurched the car forward before pulling up to make his payment. His exchange with the young male was abrupt and when his window rose with a squeal, he looked at Remi who was staring out of her raindrop-covered pane in a tense, simmering posture.

'I'm sorry,' Hingston appealed.

'It's not me you should be apologising to, Jason.'

Hingston frowned and made no remark.

The queue of cars diminished as each rolled up to the second and last window to collect their meals. As the rain thundered on the roof of his car, Hingston felt a metaphorical storm cloud encroach upon him from Remi's sphere of stroppiness.

Having endured a prolonged silence, he pulled up to the Drive Thru hatch and accepted the warm paper bag with the same impolite speed of a hungry chameleon and parked in a nearby bay.

'Well?' she prompted.

'I haven't gone to Smythe and told *him* I think he's a tosser,' Hingston replied.

'No. But I'll tell him.'

This was not the Remi of two years ago. Hingston paused, waiting for her next prompt.

'Unless you give me that burger, you idiot! And back off with the jealous ex routine!' She grabbed the bag from his lap and appeared to have forgiven him for his honest outburst. She had also apparently developed something reminiscent of Smythe's humour and Hingston wondered just how long they had been together. He quickly blotted out that consideration and focused on his steaming takeaway.

Remi spoke after bolting down the first quarter of her burger. 'The answer wasn't what you wanted, Jason; Mr and Mrs Clarke have denied us access to Robert.'

'Damn,' Hingston slapped his steering wheel.

Remi was chewing on another huge mouthful of cheese and pickle plastered, ketchup covered beef.

'What's the matter with them?' Hingston moaned. 'Robert's thirteen for God's sake; he's a teenager not a toddler!'

Remi was about to take another bite, but paused. 'Hey! I'm not sure this was such a good idea. If they've signed you off with stress then they had reason to do so. Jason, this is only making you worse.'

'It's not technically stress.' Hingston wondered if what he may say could be repeated to Smythe on a cosy night in. 'It's more to do with not getting a decent night's sleep. It doesn't stop me from having due concern about what was *my* investigation and from being able to deal with issues related to it.'

'Problems sleeping sounds like stress to me.' Remi touched his arm. She saw his eyes brighten; his expression, well-disguised, was unmistakeable and she… 'Anyway, this *teenager* is only thirteen and he's just had one of his brothers murdered and the other remains missing. It's not looking good for finding the other twin either; you *know* the issues with this case. Why would the parents want to add to the stress Robert is already experiencing? C'mon you know the effects of stress; admit it.'

Remi's forceful nature was what made her a good officer; never afraid to be direct and tackle issues head on. However, in *this* context, where Hingston could not reveal why he believed Robert Clarke would have important information for the investigation, her forceful nature was aggravating.

'C'mon put yourself in their shoes, Jason.' She blinked at him insistently.

'Okay.' Hingston resigned himself to defeat and snatched at a couple of chips. If Robert Clarke was to remain out of bounds there had to be another way around this perplexing puzzle and he pessimistically hoped that the Embling-Clarke pattern would not continue.

Chapter Thirteen
Boot Buckles and Old Laces

Hingston tied the laces of his walking boots with a sharp tug. It had been a long haul to reach his destination and the boot of his car was again full with his suitcase. The anxiety he experienced on discovering the Clarkes had refused access to Robert was now transforming into energised anticipation.

The inspiration for his walk was Remi. After he dropped her home in the early hours of Thursday morning he thought more about her advice. As such, he was "putting himself in the shoes" of the Emblings and his location was Newton St Cyres. Given, he had tweaked the meaning of Remi's advice, but it was a fantastic opportunity to give himself a positive focus on the investigation and get him out walking; a double whammy of stress relief.

Hingston had engaged himself in online research ahead of his visit, but the photographs were a poor prelude to this pretty patch of unspoilt England. He had taken an instant liking to Newton St Cyres as he entered by the winding Devonshire road which was flanked with far reaching rolling countryside. The mid-afternoon sun was flooding the fields with a dazzling radiance and swallows danced along the hedgerows. Even the car park he was stood in now was quaint and easy on the eye.

As Hingston beheld the colourful masses of honeysuckle which decorated the cottage gardens adjoining the car park, he inhaled their heady, hypnotic aroma which hung in the air.

To his left loomed the church of St Cyr and St Julitta, a dominant, robust stone giant seated upon a hillside throne with its thirteenth century tower reaching towards the Creator. Its powerful presence continued to draw mortal eyes up to the heavens and the clock face reliably recorded the minutes and hours of the centuries like a mute, knowledgeable watchman to whom the seasons and life cycles merged into one continuous stream of repetition.

Hingston strode from the car park, around and up a winding lane towards the church. He climbed the craggy stone steps and arrived in the densely populated graveyard; the lasting reminder of Newton St Cyres' bygone golden age of farming, mining, paper making, blacksmithing and boot making. Somewhere amongst the earliest rows and the subsequently chaotic, crammed placements of long passed parishioners would lay the young Charles Embling who remained separated from his lost twin George and his brother John. Hingston trod along the narrow stony path which had borne the footsteps of countless vivacious newlyweds, christening parties, sombre funeral marches and Sabbath congregations on bright days like today, in sodden, dank conditions and through autumn debris, ice and snow.

As he approached the small entrance porch and solid wooden double doors, he visualised one of them flying open as Henry Cole burst out in a delusional fit of hysteria following his false confession to the murder of Charles.

The heavy doors were closed and held together by an ice cold, black lacquered latch which required a firm twist of the wrist to lift. The door opened with ease and Hingston stepped into the cool, lofty, religious receptacle.

The air was absent of any mustiness or similar fragrance associated with old churches, so much so that its absence was noticeable and surprising. It was as if the building had failed to age and had encapsulated a world without time. A white arched ceiling sheltered the golden brown pews below with the comforting appearance of protective angel wings. Chunky rays of light shimmered like metallic mist through tall windows and between carved stone arches to create a series of soft spotlights on the smooth stone floor.

Behind the altar, a magnificent stained glass window kaleidoscopically depicted a quintet of saints. Saint Cyr shared a quarter pane with his mother, Saint Julitta, and above them was the word "Endurance". Indeed, a lot had been endured by the parishioners of Newton St Cyres over the centuries including two occurrences of the plague, the untimely losses of Charles, George and John Embling and those who were sacrificed to World War One and Two.

Hingston sat a row back from the front pew and imagined the Emblings at church service on the emotional morning of the 9th of December 1866 when Henry Cole played havoc. At least no mentally disturbed persons had falsely confessed to the murder of Daniel Clarke, Hingston thought.

His considerations were interrupted by the sound of movement at the rear of the church. A hollow, wooden clonking sound and scraping noise sounded three times and then stopped.

Hingston turned around. He was alone. There was a children's area to the far right corner of the church and a door leading to the tower to the left. Everything was still and quiet. Perplexed, he faced back to the altar.

Two thuds reverberated around the empty monumental structure. He turned again and stared to the back of the church. Was it coming from the tower?

A sense of an unidentified presence unnerved Hingston and he rose from his pew to leave. Above the pulpit he noticed a golden dove with outspread wings and it shone with an evangelical glow of deep yellow gold. A further hollow clonk from the immaculate solitude sped him to the door.

As he placed his fingers on the ring of the door latch, he heard a rush of footsteps outside on the stony path. Someone else around. He sighed and smiled.

'Jasper! Jasper!' a high pitched voice called outside.

That name again! Hingston gripped the sturdy metal latch and pulled. The door wouldn't open.

'Jasper!' the voice called and more footsteps were heard.

He heaved at the door and it flew open into the church, clattering and squeaking as Hingston released his grasp and ran out through the porch. The footsteps were fading to the right and Hingston pursued them up the steep gradient that led to the back of the church.

At the rear of the tower the narrow path continued upwards and through the gravestones towards trees and a gate. The sun was beating down on the dusty stone path and Hingston's eyes squinted as he stood still and scanned for the person who had been calling for Jasper. He could make out the movement of someone or something close to the gate under the shade of the trees. Someone waving? Someone beckoning? He took a step forward and as he did, the shadiness was erased by the sun. The gate and the trees became well-lit just like the rest of the churchyard. The same hypnotic fragrance from the cottage gardens suspended itself across Hingston's path, as pungent as it was when he had stood next to the blooms. He stared ahead. Nobody was there.

Hingston turned around and checked for movement in the grounds. The sea of tombstones lent itself well to imagined motion *and* to hiding. He saw no one and heard only the call of a solitary songbird. Disconcerted, Hingston made his way back down the path in the direction of the village. At the church porch he stopped.

The double doors were now shut. He hurried past and descended the sloping lane that led back towards the car park.

There was tranquillity in the air at the foot of the hill which put Hingston at ease. He headed toward the main road which flowed with minimal Friday afternoon traffic and made his way round to a cluster of "chocolate box" style thatched cottages painted in shades of marshmallow pink and white. They adjoined the calm Shuttern Brook which reflected Amazonian green foliage and splatterings of sunlight above the amber-brown pebbles. Hingston stood on the tiny brick built bridge and leaned on the iron balustrades as many persons, including the Emblings, may have done before him. A pause later he continued up the meandering lane between the cottages and out into the fields where only the sounds of grasshoppers and birdsong broke the silence with their timeless music.

Hingston imagined the era of the Emblings; the simplicity and the slower pace of life. He pictured a scene of overcrowded cob cottages, now long since demolished, and a few wealthier homes scattered sparsely across the unspoilt panorama, all of which hummed with life and in which the next generation grew into the trade of the generation before. The flimsy newspaper cutting with its bedazzling proclamation of Kallensee's adrenaline filled amazements suddenly came to life with so much more promise and intrigue than Hingston had experienced previously. Momentarily, its psychedelic exuberance blotted out Hingston's memory of the tents of iniquity and he found himself looking over a hedgerow into a grassy meadow. His eyes hurried about the long, wispy blades, the nodding, crispy seed heads and the splayed, flowery florets and he felt a homely recognition of the expanse.

A child's laughter carried on the breeze and Hingston saw the hairs on his arm move in a wave like the meadow grasses. He turned his head to the direction from which the laughter originated and waited for the cry of "Jasper". Nothing followed until down the hill came running a young boy with his father in pursuit. They were out enjoying the countryside just as Hingston was, just as whichever of the Embling children had once torn freely through a grassy meadow just like this, maybe even this very one.

The remainder of Hingston's walk took him back towards the village, along a stretch of the Shuttern Brook. He gazed into its refreshing clarity and saw two small Dace darting along near to the sunlit surface. Their blue backs were as silken arrow heads flying through an aqueous sky above a golden desert made of tiny polished stones which shone in shades of sepia, fawn and yellow brown. Hingston imagined the sweet, invigorating taste of stream water splashed on his lips and face to cool and energise him on a warm day such as today.

Then, as swift as two drops of dye passing from a pipette into water and saturating it with a startling vibrancy, Hingston found himself staring into a deep trough of water which reflected luminous shades of red and blue. He looked up from the trough and realised with horror that he was stood within the familiar, flamboyant circus ring. It was daytime and the mellow notes of sawdust filled his lungs and the shrill sound of a tambourine stormed into his ears. He looked about for its source and a tall, slender, middle-aged, blond man ran into the ring and commanded attention like a stunning show stallion.

There was no surge of applause or an almighty cheer, but the man was fully dressed in his costumery: close fitting red and yellow trousers, a made up face and a muscular torso which displayed tribal inspired tattoos. As the tambourine continued to barely withstand the violent shaking of his wrist, his rehearsal exploded into life with a single, one-armed somersault. He landed robustly on his feet with a dull thud and a gasp of sawdust arising around his toes. He hurled the tambourine into the air and somersaulted three more times towards the centre of the ring.

Hingston expected him to catch the tambourine on completing his breathtaking display of strength and agility, but he did not. Instead, a tender hand plucked the wooden ring of silver discs from the air as though it were a wreath of feathers, and with tambourine shimmering, she performed a running jump into the arms of the man.

He spun her like a propeller above his head until they came to a sharp stop with her smooth, pale legs resting along his shoulders in the position of the splits and she joyously shook the tambourine with her arms outstretched above her head. Her blonde hair remained softly pinned back, her cheeks were flushed with makeup and her lips were painted scarlet red. Her beauty and *her* presence made Hingston's heart race.

Their rehearsal was only just beginning, Hingston realised, as his eyes remained fixed on the girl who was wearing blue and crimson satin and who was so clearly full of life and happiness; a scene which somehow manipulated his heart as deeply as that of the night of her attack.

The man grasped the top of her calves firmly and lifted her up whilst she remained in the same elastic-like, muscle-testing pose. He forced her upwards as if he were weight lifting and upon releasing her legs he ducked backwards and she landed in front of him with her feet precisely together before performing a sweeping courtesy.

Hingston clapped in admiration but the pair were unable to hear and oblivious to his presence.

The man took a pace to the right and bowed with a smile and they quickly parted company, the man running to the left and the girl to the right.

Hingston lost sight of them both to the canvas and glanced down at his feet whilst he waited for their return. The sawdust shone and to his surprise his feet were bare. He frowned and the sawdust glowed astonishingly before the colour drained away and he felt faint. To steady himself, he took a step forward and bent his knees. His clarity of vision returned and to his terror the sawdust was now thirty or forty feet below and he was stood on a small plinth. A rope was stretched tightly from his plinth to another on the opposite side of the ring. Halfway across the rope was the tall, blond man. He had no pole for purposes of balance, but used his arms to distribute his mass away from his ankles and to in turn reduce any tipping whilst making his path to the opposite plinth.

On the opposite plinth stood the beautiful Circassian girl and her eyes were focused on the man in whom she unquestionably held the utmost confidence. In less than a minute he had reached the comparative safety of her plinth and Hingston exhaled in relief. The girl effortlessly mounted the man's shoulders for the return passage along the high wire.

The pair did not smile as they made their way back to the centre of the rope, but their eyes gleamed with a brightness that sang of both enjoyment and fear and their pupils were wildly dilated.

Hingston stared into the eyes of the girl and the thumping of his heart travelled upwards into his throat. As she neared, her pupils became wider and blacker and Hingston found himself staring at a starry night sky. Within moments the stars were replaced with the lit canvas of the tent and when he shot his eyes downwards he caught sight of his own bare feet upon the thick rope.

The ring below was well lit with gaudy, vibrant colours all around the golden sawdust. An over brimming audience sat in thick silence through awe and anticipation.

Hingston had no control over his feet. He knew they were not really his own because they were tanned and tendons poked out with an unusual appearance of strength. The big toe and the second toe were twisted either side of the rope and he felt a warm scratchiness chaffing at his skin. Each footstep was steadily placed along the rope and he swayed minimally from side to side.

The air was warm, his mouth was dry and he felt his blood pulsating around his body. He looked straight ahead and there on the plinth was the girl with her scarlet lips. He felt unnaturally strong and he recognised the scene from the rehearsal he had earlier witnessed; upon reaching the girl he was to lift her onto his shoulders and carry her back to the other side.

Without warning his whole being was engulfed with an overbearing feeling of dread and he tightened his grip on the rope between his toes. His heel trembled once and his ankle felt hot. With his arms curved downwards he placed his left foot one step further onto the rope and he saw the girl's lower lip part from the top. His foot pushed firmly against the rope and the sore, hardened skin between his toes stuck to the dry fibres. He brought his right foot forward and a pain in his ankle ricocheted up to his knee.

As he winced, the girl slowly opened her mouth and a cry from the audience was emitted like a sonic boom before a terrifying silence plugged his ears.

He felt his body sway too much to his right. With the same reliability as an aircraft's artificial horizon he could tell he was dangerously side tilting, falling painlessly into the air until his stiffened left leg hit against the rope and the inner side of his thigh dug into its tensed fibres, cutting and peeling his skin down to the curve of his inner knee. He had been spun upside down and he watched the girl, crouched upon her plinth, grasping at its edge with her tiny hands. Her mouth was open in shock and her eyes bulged as she watched him plummet. She became smaller and smaller. The circus colours raced before his eyes until with a hideous cracking sensation all went black.

As if he were semi-conscious within a horrifying dream Hingston failed to break out of this torment. He saw the blond man lying face down. His head was flattened from the front and the golden colour of the sawdust was flooded with claret which slowly seeped under his crumpled body and through his yellow and red trousers.

The audience was in a state of hysteria, some persons running into the ring to look closer at the gory spectacle, others ran out of the tent and most were frozen to their seats. A lone horse had broken free and galloped across the ring before rearing up at one of the equestriennes who bravely tried to control him from the ground.

The performers had rushed in from behind the canvasses to attend to the blond, unfortunate man and they held back the audience from the scene.

The beautiful Circassian girl shook like the tambourine as she climbed down the ladder attached to her plinth and ran in desperation towards the centre of the ring with her bare feet pounding the sawdust.

It was the stout, well dressed gentleman who grabbed hold of the young, devastated wreck as she fought against him to reach the lifeless mass of tissue and broken bones that had smashed upon the sawdust. 'Stay away from your father. Stay away from your father!' he ordered the girl who tussled in his arms and cried and gasped her grief into the scene of panic and ruin. And once again, all went black as though the curtain was drawn upon this heart wrenching catastrophe.

Stunned and shaking with a sensation of emptiness filling his lungs, Hingston found himself staring solemnly into Shuttern Brook. A lonely Dace passed beneath his gaze and his thoughts of the vulnerable Circassian girl flickered in his moist eyes. He pictured the spangled world of Kallensee's Great Circus which boasted about fantastic wonders but which used all its bedazzling magic to shroud a world of danger and darkness behind a cloak as thick as tent canvas.

He resumed his path back to the car under the watchful realm of the church, sickened by the experience of death and desolation. The young girl's face presided in his mind.

* * *

As he drove back along the A377, he attempted to focus his mind away from the circus tragedy and turned his thoughts to Miss Eliza Norma Tolcher. Hingston had formed the opinion that the forty-six-year-old spinster was a simple woman. She was a basket weaver, not a woman of the church, but a Druid; not a heathen or a witch, but a woman who put her faith in nature and its secret powers. Inspector Bell considered the theft of the silver pocket watch to be Miss Tolcher's motive for the murder of Charles Embling. The wider community and indeed the press created a furore about the holly branch and the acorns which Miss Tolcher admitted she had laid at the site of Charles' death. They claimed that this was part of a witchcraft ritual.

Indeed, superstition in 1860s rural Devon had not dwindled sufficiently to prevent such accusations from being made, particularly when crops failed or cattle died. The murder of a boy attracted even more locals to jump on the witchcraft bandwagon. Hingston had been surprised to read an article printed in the Western Times only three years before the murder, in which a farmer approached a "white witch" for advice due to his fear that the loss of his possessions was a result of witchcraft.

Hingston's phone rang on the hands free.

'Jason! How's the journey been? Are you almost here?'

'About twenty minutes,' Hingston replied. 'But thought I'd grab us a takeaway first,' he proposed.

'Since I knew you were coming I've prepared us a bit of a treat!'

Hingston fought with mixed feelings. The "bit of a treat" sounded very inviting, but the collection of a takeaway came with the opportunity to visit Bayard's Cove Fort, something Hingston had been looking forward to for several days.

Zack decided to fill the silence left by Hingston. 'Well, you may think your uncle a bit foolish splashing out on two lobsters totalling six pounds in weight, but they're absolute beauties and what's wrong with a bit of frivolity from time to time, eh!' His laughter boomed into the car.

Uncle Zack's words bounced around Hingston's mind with a degree of familiarity as he juggled thoughts of the elderly woman and the two large lobsters. 'I think that's more than a bit of a treat!' Hingston finally exclaimed. 'I'll see you soon.'

The call ended and Hingston smiled; not about the lobster, but about Uncle Zack's inadvertent memory jogger. At last, the words of the elderly woman fell back into place: "*foolishness* and *frivolity* are friends of your foe and your foe will use them to get away with a *felony*".

'And what better place for foolishness and frivolity?' Hingston said with excitement. 'A CIRCUS!' And the significance of the elderly woman's words ignited his mind, creating a flaming spotlight upon the felonious, bearded red-head.

Chapter Fourteen
In the Depths of Castle Wood

At ten a.m. the next morning, Hingston reached Cadbury and saw that the parish had largely been forgotten by the modern world. As Uncle Zack had informed him last night, the Industrial Revolution had long ago succeeded in stealing away Cadbury's parishioners to pursue lives of opportunity in towns and cities. A token few residences remained amongst miles of rolling farmland, and the only evidence that there had once been a thriving community was the church of St Michael and All Angels which stood tall amongst the trees.

Hingston parked up just off the main road. It felt strange that there were no quaint rows of cottages and thatch. The atmosphere was one of emptiness and a certain sadness presided over the land as he walked down the narrow Milk Lane towards the church.

Amongst the gravestones grew hundreds of tall-stemmed daisies, all gazing upwards at Hingston as he found a path through the grounds. It was not just the bold yellow eyes with their white lashes that made him feel like he was being watched. The mossy, weather-worn, sloping and slanting stones displayed the surnames familiar to him from Inspector Bell's file. There, only feet away, was Mary Elizabeth Cudlip, 1839-1885; the woman who had rushed to Constable Heale on the 3rd of December 1866 having witnessed Miss Tolcher laying acorns and a branch of holly, an action she interpreted as evidence that Miss Tolcher had sacrificed Charles to the Devil.

'Can I help you?' a deep voice called with a broad Devonshire lilt.

Hingston jumped which prompted a swift apology from the unshaven, fifty-something-year-old who was wearing a broad rimmed, floppy hat.

'Just taking in the sights of Cadbury,' said Hingston.

The man came into view with a hoe and a barrow. 'There's very little left of the parish nowadays. I do the church gardening. Don't know much of the history.' He spoke with a puckered up nose and squinted his piggy eyes suspiciously at Hingston. 'Of course, there's Cadbury Castle. You may have seen the signs for it. Iron Age hill fort,' he shouted as if Hingston were deaf. 'Shares the same name as another in Somerset which has been linked to the legends of King Arthur. You know, dragons, knights, secret caves. Course there's none of that *here*, but the views are worth the walk.' The man gestured with a stumpy finger which was stained by the russet soil and directed Hingston out of the churchyard and off to the right.

Hingston could not take his mind off Miss Tolcher. He was intent on finding *her* cave; a *real* one. 'Do you know how to get to Castle Wood?'

Hingston received vague directions and made his way back to Milk Lane, leaving the lone gardener to his chores.

When he reached the top of Cadbury Castle the views gave him a perfect panorama from which to ponder the route taken by the Emblings. To his right, as advised by the gardener, was Castle Wood, a dense, dark green mass, detached and obscure without a guidepost or a trodden path with which to set a starting point. Undeterred from his investigative plight, Hingston headed toward the wood.

A few yards into Castle Wood's sun dappled undergrowth the air changed. It was cooler and the ferns, foliage and bark exuded a sweet, fresh fragrance as the forest respired.

Hingston pressed ahead, stopped and looked back. The path he had taken lay still and silent. A bright radiance dazzled at the edge of the field that could just be seen between the shaded tree trunks. As he took a deep breath, a burst of excitement surged through his chest. He imagined this blooming green entrance encrusted with a sparkling haw frost and lit by a silver December light. Hingston's chosen route was designed to take him to the centre, to the depths of Castle Wood, and he wondered whether any of his footfalls would retrace those of Inspector Bell.

He pulled his compass from his pocket, set it to northeast and proceeded along an untouched carpet of last autumn's remaining leaves and twigs. Clusters of spongy toadstools with the appearance of miniature Chinamen and tiny parasols had erupted near the roots of ancient oaks.

The geography began to change. The ground dropped away and small hillocks had to be negotiated. Hingston's boots thumped on rocks embedded in the sloping ground and ivy and bracken crunched as he trudged through increasingly thicker undergrowth. He watched his feet trampling the plant life which had knitted itself into an almost impassable mass and he glanced up at the towering trees.

Hingston stopped for breath. The wood fell silent. An overwhelming sense of timelessness rose like a mist. Fearing a loss of bearings, he studied the maze of ancient tree trunks. The canopy above was so thick that the light had turned a milky grey. He felt the trees oozing opposition, colluding with the tangled vegetation that tugged at his feet to trip, tire and confuse anyone who dare explore the secrets guarded within the depths.

Perhaps it was the murder of Charles Embling that forced Castle Wood to grow so dense, to protect itself from future human interference?

The silence became too much to bear. He gripped his compass which read northeast. He had not strayed off course. He stepped forward, snapping a twig. The sound resonated outwards and stirred not a single bird or animal in the wood. The isolation was suffocating.

For thirty-five minutes he stamped and pushed his way through the defiant woodland, up and down steep gradients. Nothing resembled a cave or a Druid relic. His cotton shirt was moist with sweat and droplets of perspiration were emerging on his upper lip. He pulled a bottle of water from the pouch on the side of his rucksack and downed half its volume. Unsurprisingly, his mobile had no signal. It was now one thirty.

Onwards he strode. Finally, he sighted something of interest. He hurried over, catching his trouser legs in the bracken. A series of moss covered rocks positioned in a circle were sat on the top of a small mound. Clearly, the ring had not been formed by nature and it had lain unmoved for many generations given its embedded appearance.

Hingston felt optimistic that this discovery related to Miss Tolcher. He studied the weathered mysteries without entering the circle and questioned their intended purpose. Were they significant to prayer? To life? To death?

He ran his fingers over the patches of the soft, fluffy moss and the cold, craggy rock. He looked at his compass and was taken aback. It indicated he had strayed off to the west, but he had been travelling consistently northeast. Puzzled, Hingston surveyed his surroundings. There was nothing to evidence his direction of travel. Perplexed, he adjusted his compass and continued.

About fifty yards ahead he had to negotiate a sharp slope downwards and he leaned back into his heels, preparing to slip and skid his way into the fern filled basin. His last few steps down were hurried, as if he had been pushed, and before him he noticed a sizeable piece of granite laying flat amongst the foliage, almost obscured by forest debris.

Intrigued, Hingston lifted a large stick from the undergrowth and swept the debris to one end of the stone, revealing a dozen unrecognisable, carved letters, each about five inches in height and they were presented in a circular formation. Some resembled the English alphabet, but they were impossible to decipher. He stared at the simplistic, angular symbols and ran his hand over the cool granite which was rough from a fine coating of decayed organic particles. He felt exhilarated. He pressed his index finger into the deep, channelled groove which looked like an arrow head and brushed out more debris. A beetle scuttled away post-haste into the shelter of nearby undergrowth.

An impromptu rustling of dried leaves outside of the basin caught his attention. It was the only sound he had heard since entering the wood that was created by a source other than himself. Hingston looked upwards from his crouched position by the tablet. His eyes darted between the tree trunks and the mottled foliage between them became as confusing as a hall of mirrors. He felt vulnerable and *watched*. The rustling sounded again. It was louder and Hingston scanned the perimeter of the basin. A gust of wind whooshed down the slope towards him, chilled his eyes and carried the debris back over the granite tablet. It skimmed his hand and he observed the last few leaves drift into the ferns. His ears throbbed. His eyes followed the direction of the gust, towards the opposite rising side of the basin, where a dark, craggy mass of rocks framed a black, unknown space.

Hingston remained still by the tablet for several minutes, waiting for someone to appear. Nothing came. Glancing about himself he neared his target. The feathery ferns clung to his trouser legs with each step he took. *This was* a cave! A cave of moderate proportions; about five feet wide and six feet high at the mouth and the dimly lit entrance extended into pitch blackness of a depth unknown.

Hingston located his torch in his rucksack. He hesitated, listening for any movement. The wood lay silent and the cave was mute. He stepped inside and shone his torch. The rugged ceiling sparkled with dampness and as Hingston made his way in, the temperature dropped and the cave's mouldy smell became intense. His heart pounded as he thought of the bitter cold of December 1866. If this *were* Miss Tolcher's cave, there were numerous ledges upon which the bloodied knife could have sat.

Shallowly breathing the dank, heavy air, Hingston continued. His torch lit the moist stones at the back of the cave and a swathe of disappointment passed over him. This was it; a damp, cold, impersonal space.

The anonymous note he had read in Inspector Bell's murder file seemed to promise so much more, but of course *so much* time had passed. Miss Tolcher was arrested and hanged when many of those buried in the grounds of Cadbury church were still in the throes of youth, and when some hadn't even been born. Only Hingston's recent discoveries made them seem alive once again.

In resignation, Hingston pursed his lips together and hoped there may be another cave to find. He stepped backwards, sweeping his torchlight. His heel hit against a protruding rock and he tripped, stumbling to his right, his boot slamming into a ledge.

Hingston regained his balance, gasped for breath and his hands shook. On moving his foot from the ledge, a gentle sound of stone hitting stone was heard. He illuminated the ledge and pressed his hand on the rock that adjoined it. It moved!

He slid the rock away from the ledge and onto the floor. A pungent, rotting smell emanated and it made him gag.

Wincing, he covered his nose and mouth with his shirt sleeve, flashed his torchlight into the small void and stared. It was impossible to identify the blackened mass which was slotted tightly inside. However, he could see that its shape was angular. The stench continued to make him feel sick. He used his torch to poke at the unknown article. The outer was soft, but not far beneath its soggy surface, it felt solid.

Hingston propped his torch against his rucksack. With both hands he gripped the chilled object, holding his breath as his fingers sunk in. A few harsh tugs were required to ease it free. The dimensions surprised him. It was similar in size to the musical box, but significantly lighter and a long roll of leather was responsible for its spongy surface.

Hingston followed his torchlight out of the cave. The sweet, woodland air was refreshing. He laid the object on the granite tablet and rolled away three feet of decayed and mouldy leather to reveal a rusted tin box. Stood amongst the silent ferns, he stared in amazement; his belief renewed that he may have found Miss Tolcher's cave.

He looked about and with an uneasy pang of self-consciousness he pulled out his groundsheet, wrapped the tin and bundled it into his rucksack.

* * *

Uncle Zack's gardening gloves lay discarded on the patio, speckled with tiny shards of metal like casualties of war. Hingston squinted in the sunlight. Beneath an inner wrapping of chilled leather, bundles and wadges of papers parcelled up with string filled the tin to near capacity. They were discoloured and flimsy, but the handwriting on them was in English and appeared generally legible. He knelt as he read the words "blackberry leaf" and "cowslip".

Hingston covered the dining room table with the papers and read the first one; a record of a herbal remedy given to treat a blocked nose, namely elderflowers and peppermint, equal parts, in boiling water. The patient recovered in four days and a line of praise was written to the oak trees. The author of these records *had* to be Miss Tolcher.

The likelihood of making such a discovery finally hit Hingston with complete astonishment. Previously undiscovered evidence from a Victorian murder investigation was being pulled into the present. And into the present they were all converging at one point: Hingston.

He read on. Miss Tolcher had retained records of natural treatments, prayers, star gazing observations and notable events which together formed a diary, an insight into the life of an outsider.

He felt sadness and guilt on behalf of the Victorian police as he began to understand Miss Tolcher. He knew that no member of her community, or the police, had taken the time, the interest or displayed the courage to find out who she really was. There was no doubt that Miss Tolcher was educated. It was simply her philosophy that was unconventional and misunderstood. She treated few patients it seemed, which did not come as a surprise given the views of the majority of the Cadbury parishioners. She did, however, self-medicate and cared for injured animals. She recorded the change of the seasons, any unexpected shifts in the weather and was clearly observant, for anything she considered an exception to the norm she passed comment upon. This, to Hingston's excitement, included events in the last few months of her freedom, which he realised the moment he read the words "may the traveller boy be borne into love and comfort in the Otherworld". This must have been her prayer for Charles Embling.

No sooner had he read these words, his mobile rang. It was Remi.

'Jason. Robert Clarke's gone missing.'

It was the words he had been expecting, but not wanting to hear.

The call was short and to the point. What more was there to say? Hingston was grateful, for Remi did not have to tell him. The tip-off gave him confidence that she trusted his soundness of mind. The parallel between the Clarkes and the Emblings was now *unquestionable* and it spurred him on in his review of Miss Tolcher's records.

The delicate paper still felt cold from its protracted hibernation in Castle Wood. Hingston continued to take each annotated bundle in turn. None were dated and it was difficult to tell whether Miss Tolcher had organised the contents in any sort of order. The next related to "a fair wanderer" to whom horehound leaves were given for "wounds" to self and to "Gino".

Hingston's eyes pinballed between the words "wounds", "fair wanderer" and the name "Gino". He felt cold and looked at the tin box which sat on the sideboard behind the table. The blackness of the metal spilled out into the room like molten tar and he tried to close his eyes but they were fixed on the growing darkness which was billowing out towards him. His ears filled with the scream before he saw her helpless, terrified face, begging him for help and as he looked, the oxidised blood shone out from her cheek and her brow.

The furious, flaming red-head turned to Hingston as he had once before and his clenched teeth protruded from his thin, overstretched, blood-drained lips. He pulled back his right arm like an archer reaching full tension on his bow, his white-knuckled fist grasping the belt. The buckle cut through the air towards Hingston at tremendous velocity and as he ducked and gasped he found himself back at the dining room table unscathed. His heart was racing from a sudden revelation.

The "fair wanderer" *had* to be the beautiful Circassian girl. His night terrors and visions were dovetailing together with reality and his investigative deductions. He had ascertained that Kallensee's Circus *was* close enough to Cadbury for one of its performers to meet with Miss Tolcher and be given treatment for her wounds. Wounds she had received from a fiercely violent man with a beard; a man who could also be described as "tall with whiskers". Possibly the same man Miss Tolcher claimed had been inside her house; the man who therefore deposited Mr Embling's pocket watch; the man who if in possession of the watch had taken it from the Embling twins and who therefore most probably murdered Charles? Maybe the anonymous note contained within Inspector Bell's file from "J.B." was penned by this evil, bearded creature? Could it be Mr J. Bibbings, the Acting Manager of Kallensee's Great Circus?

Hingston's head was reeling with excitement. The bearded red-head *was* the murderer, not Miss Tolcher; he had framed her! He was entirely confident of that now. But who was Gino? If Gino was also wounded, he must have been present at the time of the attack on the girl.

'The whispering!' Hingston exclaimed. He remembered the menagerie tent. When the red-head entered there was whispering and a candle light was extinguished. And the footfalls in the sawdust! Hingston remembered. There must have been somebody with the girl in the tent who he had not seen. Perhaps it was Gino? Could Gino be one of the twins?

Hingston stood up. He needed to put a halt to his whirring head. He wanted to try to work out how his new found evidence could help solve the Clarkes' case, but he felt unable to concentrate.

The musical box was upstairs; his equivalent of a strong brandy and now, a trusted travelling companion. He *needed* to hear its music. He hurried up to the bright guest room where the red bed linen was as bold and welcoming as ever.

He scooped up the musical box and took a brief peer out of the window. The cricket pitch was an energising emerald green and beyond the road was the River Dart.

In amongst the holidaymakers he noticed a small, dark, familiar figure. He watched her cross the road towards the cricket pitch.

'How much do you know?' he questioned her through the window pane.

She continued along the path adjacent to the pitch which ran parallel to the river and which was largely obscured by the boundary hedges. Her speed was constant and her silky grey bun reminded Hingston of a small puff of steam from the Dartmouth Railway engines. She was heading into town, away from Uncle Zack's house. Hingston counted ahead to predict where she would be seen again in-between the gaps and dips of the random hedgerow: privet, laurel, privet, privet, *bun*, laurel, laurel, *bun*, laurel, privet, laurel, *face*! She was staring straight at him. *Eyeballing* him. There was no mistaking the instantaneous about turn she must have performed to look up, over a low point in the hedge and directly into Uncle Zack's first floor bedroom window where Hingston was standing.

He didn't turn away and he certainly didn't wave. He returned her stare which despite the distance, was intense and unsettling.

There was a heavy clunk from downstairs as the front door opened. Hingston hesitated to prevent himself from heading to the landing. He kept his eyes on the elderly woman's eyes which appeared as motionless as stone, but as charged as an electric storm. He listened for Uncle Zack, for the front door to close and for his voice to boom up the stairs, but there was silence.

Hingston clasped the musical box and the elderly woman lowered her gaze to the ground floor of the house, to the front door.

'Zack?' he called as he continued to watch the old woman.

There was no response.

Unable to resist any longer, Hingston turned his head towards the landing. Everything was in order, silent and still. He glanced back out of the window. She remained there, statuesque, staring at the door. He felt scared. Tactical raids and unpredictable altercations had instilled in him a confidence and level-headedness that until this point had been reliable and self-assuring.

He placed the musical box on the bed and made his way to the landing. The front door was wide open and the warm evening light gave the carpet an inviting lustre. He descended the stairs, his eyes and ears working double time to detect any presence in the house. There was no one. His attention moved to the front door. To his disbelief, the locks were protruding from the door; someone had relocked it after opening it into the hall, but the keys were nowhere to be seen.

As he stepped into the doorway, the evening sun began to brighten and as he strained to look beyond the front garden towards the elderly woman, a heavy, golden mist descended. He blinked repeatedly and the shimmering hue began to rapidly condense and coagulate into an endless sea of wispy grass. He gazed, dumbfounded, before stepping forward into the luscious meadow of his mind. He did not look back into the hallway. Instead, he surveyed the delicate blades and feathery seed heads, watching for the curly haired boy who he now knew to be one of the Embling twins. Over to the right he noticed a figure and as he made his way through the thick, fluffy grass, the figure came into full definition. The moment he recognised the blonde hair and scarlet lips it stopped.

The meadow was gone and the girl was gone. He was stood on the pavement outside the house, facing the cricket pitch. He was staring at the exact spot where the elderly woman had been staring back at him, but she was nowhere to be seen.

Chapter Fifteen
A Timely Assessment

The hours between eight p.m. and midnight flowed like magicians' silk and a tangible energy ran through the air that filled the house.

Inspiration gradually replaced Hingston's fears about the afternoon's events involving the elderly woman. He continued to read Miss Tolcher's records and felt renewed, as though he had ingested a carefully measured remedy.

By nine p.m. the news of Robert Clarke's disappearance was no longer a burden to Hingston. Instead, he felt focused, ready for the next phase of the Clarke investigation, and when Uncle Zack returned from his day's visit to Aunt Beryl, Hingston did not delay in telling him why.

'Evidence from eighteen sixty-six! Evidence missed by Inspector Bell and examined by me this evening,' he boasted with a broad grin, lounging back with his hands interlocked behind his head.

'Goodness me!' Uncle Zack walked over to the table, pleased to see signs that Hingston was returning to his confident self.

'These papers,' Hingston passed his hand over the table, 'belonged to *Miss Eliza Norma Tolcher*. By sheer luck, chance, fate, whatever you want to call it, I found them in *her* cave in Castle Wood. They are significant for *two* reasons.'

Uncle Zack nodded, his eyes wide in disbelief.

'Firstly, I am now entirely confident that Miss Tolcher was innocent. She did not murder Charles Embling. And secondly, there's a record here,' Hingston picked up one of the papers and balanced it on his fingers, 'which I will read out to you.'

'Go on.'

'Newcomer this morning. Well dressed, but young and unaccompanied where he should have been for a boy so small. Would not speak and hurried away so as to disappear as soon as he had arrived.'

Uncle Zack frowned. 'You're gonna have to explain that one, Jason.'

'You remember I mentioned over lobster, that my reinvestigation of Inspector Bell's file revealed that John Embling, the younger brother of the Embling twins, subsequently ran away from home?'

'Yes. I see! You think Miss Tolcher saw him. Makes sense.'

'Yes. Call it a hunch, but Miss Tolcher's papers indicate she was a very observant woman. I'd already considered that John Embling may have headed either to the site of Charles' murder or in search of George, but this appears to evidence that this small eight-year-old did make it to Cadbury, for whatever purpose.'

'It's very interesting, but why are you so excited by it? What's the significance?'

'Today, Robert Clarke, the younger brother of the twins was reported missing. It's another one of these uncanny parallels; repeats of history that keep occurring throughout the Clarke case.'

'And?'

'If the young brother, John Embling, was sighted then perhaps we can predict that Robert Clarke will be sighted also. And if he *is* sighted…'

'Then you could save him,' Uncle Zack butted in.

'Bingo!' Hingston smiled. 'We're in with a chance!'

* * *

Wednesday the 1st of June arrived more quickly than Hingston had anticipated when he diarised his Occupational Health appointment just over three weeks ago. He sat alone in the London waiting room upon terracotta coloured, open weave seats. Their solid sponge filled cushions and lumbar supports were comfortable and held Hingston in such an upright position that reading the busy notice board was almost a mandatory duty. Hingston's attention was drawn between the brightly coloured posters like he was following the random motion of a panicked fly trying to escape a small room. By the time he'd absorbed the key messages: debt, trauma incident management, domestic abuse, heart disease, knowing your limits, Chlamydia and stress, he felt very much akin to a panicked fly. Rather than looking for an exit, he scanned the walls for a clock. It was 2.59 p.m. and his appointment was at three.

The door to Patricia's office broke the silence and she called 'bye for now' to her patient who nodded and left with his hands in his pockets and with a swagger that suggested he was ready to fool the world that everything was okay. Once he was out of the waiting area, Patricia called 'Jason' in an upbeat tone.

Hingston sat down in the deep blue armchair and rested his arms on the puffed-up cushions. Patricia sat in her tapestry-effect, well-worn chair, crossed her legs and gave an encouraging smile.

Hingston stared at her burgundy red hair which was pulled tightly away from her face before exploding into a curly mass at the nape of her neck. Her emerald green, short-sleeved blouse was decorated with a string of black, glossy beads. Her blue mascara screamed of the eighties and her burgundy nails matched her hair exactly. On looking at the "size fourteen" Patricia with her black trousers and kitten-heels, he wondered whether it takes a whacky individual to psychoanalyse people or whether this is simply the type of person such a career attracts.

'You've changed your hair colour,' Hingston observed. She was platinum blonde at his previous appointment.

Patricia smiled. 'Let's talk about *you*, Jason,' she directed. 'What's changed for you since we last met?'

'My night terrors have stopped.'

Patricia looked at him intently. 'Go on,' she said.

'In the past few days I've slept through without any disturbance. They appear to have ended as suddenly as they came.'

'And what else has changed?' she questioned with an emotionless face.

'I'm not at all stressed or anxious and as you can see,' Hingston thought he would try a little psychology of his own, 'I look well and I feel well.' He smiled with a cheeky glimmer in his eyes.

Patricia stared at him and passed no comment on how he looked. His dark circles had disappeared. He had regained his usual energy which was apparent from his posture and his commanding voice; he had not forgotten to shave and his shoes were polished to an immaculate shine. But did she believe him? Perhaps she thought he was full of bravado?

He continued. 'It's as if the night terrors had never happened, I feel back to normal.'

'Let's talk about the night terrors, Jason. When we met three and a half weeks ago you spoke about a boy and a meadow.'

'Yes, I did.'

'And this boy was running through the meadow and you said he was wearing a white shirt and braces?'

Hingston nodded.

'And you felt like you were chasing him?'

'Correct.'

'And now?'

Hingston gave Patricia a blank look, but inwardly he was frowning, pondering how to answer and whether his answer would be interpreted by her in his favour or not. 'The boy has gone.'

'So the meadow remained, but the boy had run away, out of sight?'

Hingston felt this assessment was going to be hard work and questioned whether he was the one who should be assessed. 'No meadow. No boy. The night terrors have ended.'

'How did they end, Jason?' she probed.

'Like I said at my previous appointment with you, I was only remembering snippets, snippets which made no sense. It remained that way,' he lied without a hint of deceit. 'The night terrors remained illogical and then they ended. I'm none the wiser,' he added with a small raise of his eyebrows.

Patricia tilted her head to the side and pouted her lips in thought. 'How about the Clarke twins?' she asked.

Hingston felt his eyes widen minimally and was instantly annoyed with himself because micro expressions would be what Patricia was looking for. 'Yes,' he said, trying to disguise any element of concern.

'You contacted your manager, DI Brace, about them around two weeks ago. Is that right, Jason?'

'It is.'

'And did DI Brace tell you she was going to contact me about that?'

'Yes. If I recall correctly, she said I was still troubled by the case.'

'She did, Jason. What's your response to that?'

'Incorrect. I am a professional officer who is passionate about what I do. I take every case seriously and give of my all. The Clarke case has been unusual in that there's been too many unanswered questions. That doesn't mean I'm troubled by it.' Hingston took breath. 'And *because* I take a genuine interest in it and the safety of the missing boys, I put in a considered call but get accused of being troubled by the case. I think she overreacted, to be honest.' Hingston's voice was controlled but his face expressed his distaste towards Brace.

'And how are you feeling now you have stopped working on the case?'

Hingston looked Patricia straight in the eye. He felt his mobile vibrate in his trouser pocket. 'Apologies,' he raised his eyebrows. 'I'll just turn that off.' He slid his phone between his thumb and forefinger. A new text message. Smythe. Hingston shifted his eyes to the power button and pressed it. As the screen went blank his chest filled with energy. 'The past few weeks have released my anxieties,' Hingston responded to Patricia's question and avoided appearing smug. 'They've been the key to making me a better detective.'

'A better detective?' Patricia exclaimed.

'I've become more open minded,' Hingston advised, 'and that's allowed me to relax because I no longer expect *anything* to be predictable. For that reason I can roll freely with an investigation as it develops.' Hingston smiled.

Finally, Patricia allowed Hingston to see a mild smile pass over her lips. He also noticed her hazel eyes glint with a secretive contentedness much like that he observed in the eyes of the elderly woman just two afternoons previously.

* * *

On Monday afternoon Hingston seated himself in the sunshine overlooking the River Dart, near to the harbour.

'I'm surprised to find you sat here when you've been spending so much time at Bayard's Cove,' the elderly woman yet again caught Hingston unawares. She gave him a cool look from her beady, green-grey eyes which examined him rapidly.

Indeed the old lady was correct. He had frequented Bayard's Cove almost obsessively since Saturday evening's encounter by the cricket pitch. He had been determined to see her, but to no avail. Of course, he now knew that *she* had seen *him*.

'How do you know that when you haven't been about?' he snapped.

She stepped towards Hingston and eased herself down next to him. Her stick reflected dozens of spots of sunlight from the carved flowers and foliage and her eyes sparkled. 'It's curious you have taken so much interest in me,' she said.

Hingston was very aware that she had again avoided his question, but having maintained the focus on herself, he seized the moment to ask another. 'Tell me. What was Saturday evening all about when you were staring at me across the cricket pitch?'

The old lady tilted her head in the manner of a thoughtful sparrow. 'I think you must be mistaken,' she responded.

'No, madam,' Hingston jumped in. 'You were most definitely there. And what was going on with my front door?'

She looked out across the river and laughed. She was tickled by something. Her reaction was similar to the amusement that only an elderly person experiences when a child does something mundane and predictable. Perhaps that was it; she knew he would robustly disagree with her response. Or was she enjoying teasing him?

Hingston remained silent. He was determined to regain some authority and control.

She cut her laughter short and as she turned to face him, her smile began to fade. 'Sometimes you see me and sometimes you do not, but you are always looking. The question is, how reliable is your vision?'

She had done it again; floated out a consideration which could be interpreted in multiple ways. Was she speaking about his eyesight or his night terrors? Or specifically about the girl and the meadow which appeared before him on Saturday evening?

Hingston felt hot. 'My vision's good enough. You were there,' he challenged.

She remained silent.

'I know who the boy is,' he announced.

'The boy?' she echoed and her eyes glinted with a secretive contentedness.

'Yes.' Hingston had no intention to discuss the Embling twin at this stage. 'But you haven't told me who *you* are.'

The old woman glanced down at her hands. 'Neither have you,' she replied, 'and I wasn't about to ask.' A smug look was concealed by a turn of her head.

Frustrated, Hingston decided it was time to change tack. He would achieve the answer eventually. 'I've been thinking about something you said to me previously.'

Her eyes were fixed on him. He had her attention.

'You made a direct remark about a foe getting away with a felony.' Hingston raised his eyebrows to encourage her response.

'The furrows in your brow and your questioning technique tell me a lot about your career. And if I recall correctly, it was you who first spoke of criminality.' She inhaled the breeze which brushed past them from the river, keeping Hingston in brief suspense. 'I have the impression *you* should be the expert on that subject matter.' Hingston felt foxed and unnerved. Before he could reply she added, 'Even if you did make a foolish remark about the absence of crime in Devon.'

'That was intended to be a light-hearted joke.'

The elderly woman's attention was being drawn back to the river. 'I don't think you need me to explain any more about felony, my dear.' She smiled as she gazed across the sparkling blue-green expanse and her kind tone took Hingston by surprise. 'As a matter of fact, I think your problem is being eased apart with the ebb and flow of the sea.'

'Madam, how did you know I had a problem when we first met?'

'Now if you please, I shall ask you not to delay me any further. I have a boat to catch.'

Hingston noticed a Dartmouth River Cruise ticket clasped between her thumb and forefinger. Her thick nails were manicured and of medium length; pristine with a clear, shiny varnish.

She grasped her stick, levered herself to her feet and without looking at Hingston or passing polite remark she headed steadily but slowly toward the grand, glossy cruise boat.

'Why did you take an interest, madam?' Hingston called before she was out of earshot.

She paused and turned. 'Someone once did me a good turn; many moons ago that is. Maybe it was my time to do something in return.'

'So who are you helping?' Hingston called as he began to ease himself up from the bench.

No response came.

Hingston felt nauseous. He feared his time with the elderly lady was being sucked away with the same irretrievability as one recognises when the remaining litre of bath water whirlpools down the plughole. He still had a day left before returning to London. He would try to find her again.

Whilst Hingston watched the familiar bun and dreary clothing make their way onto the boat, she raised her hand which clasped the ticket and she waved it back and forth with a casual twist of her wrist. She did not look back.

The sunlight bounced off her pearlescent red nails and Hingston took a sharp intake of breath. The nail colour was new. He couldn't have overlooked this when she was sat with him? No, they had been clear and shiny. Definitely not red.

He stared at the shocking red nails which glowed brighter and fiercer. They began to tremble and one melted into a smooth flow of claret. Its colour flooded his vision for a split second and he was confronted with the flow of oxygenated blood erupting from a brow of porcelain skin. And then, with the speed of a rapid slideshow, the girl with the scarlet lips reached out with her arm, begging without words for help. The monstrous red-head threw back his shoulders and turned, a vile hatred plumed like poisonous gas from his snarling nose and his black eyes of death lay in wait in the cave of his heavy, frowning brow. The red-head stepped in front of the girl and snarled. He pulled back his right arm, gripping his thick, heavy belt and the scene darkened. Hingston fought to maintain his grasp on the scene. 'Show me more! *Please!* Show me more!' The red-head lashed forward and the curly haired boy lunged into the sordid capsule of criminality and his bellow of '*Noooooooooooo!*' harmonised with the siren of the Dartmouth cruise boat.

Short of breath, Hingston found himself staring at the sunny jetty. The elderly woman was out of sight. And that was his last encounter with her.

* * *

Now, in his Occupational Health assessment, he hoped the glint of secretive contentedness in Patricia's eyes was also a positive indication that she was satisfied with his response.

'Tell me, Jason, what has happened with the music you were hearing?'

'I know it very well now,' he confessed. 'It was always a calming mechanism after the night terrors, which as I stated earlier, have stopped.'

Patricia nodded and her burgundy red curls trembled. 'So the music has stopped as well?'

'Yes,' he smiled, visualising the musical box and its perfect, performing pins.

'Okay, good.' Patricia touched her beaded necklace which Hingston interpreted as a sign she was relaxing, enjoying the progress made and planning her closing recommendation. She jotted down a couple of notes. 'Your relationship with DI Brace, how is that?' she asked.

'Fine.' Hingston opted for a short response.

'You gave me the impression earlier that you were dissatisfied with your last conversation with her.'

'Yes, I was. But as I said, I'm a professional officer. I have put that behind me,' he nodded.

There was a moment's silence whilst Patricia and Hingston gathered their thoughts.

'Jason,' her tone was warm and reassuring. 'I'm satisfied that you have let go of your anxieties and I believe that they were related to the Clarke case.'

Hingston stared back at her with a relaxed posture. Inside, his head and his heart were racing.

'Studies suggest that when we dream we are chasing someone we are attempting to overcome a difficult task. In your case, I believe this was the Clarke investigation. The fact the night terrors and the music have stopped and you appear to be recovered, reassure me you are fit for work. I'm happy to recommend that you return to work, provided you have no further dealings with the case.'

'The murder squad are dealing with it now,' Hingston said.

'Well, that's very convenient. Shall I recommend you return to work on Sunday or is that too soon for you?'

'Sunday's fine for me.' Hingston's eyes shone with enthusiasm. 'Thank you.' As he rose from his chair he touched his trouser pocket.

Patricia noticed. 'Oh yes. You've got that text message awaiting you. Take care, Jason, and I'll see you in a fortnight just to check how you're settling back into work.'

A few feet out of the waiting room Hingston turned on his phone and tapped on Smythe's message. It was direct and devoid of any pleasantries, just like Smythe himself. Hingston smiled as he read the order: "Call me".

Chapter Sixteen
Detection and Duplicity

Hingston called from his car. Smythe was either fighting off an infection or he had recently engaged himself in a shouting fit, for his booming voice was quietened by the presence of an unhealthy rasping noise.

'We've got someone in custody. He was in possession of a bag that matches the P.E. bag belonging to Daniel Clarke. He's a vagrant believed to be from the local area. Kicked off and assaulted an officer when questioned about the bag. He's sobering up in a cell as we speak. Do you know the latest on Robert Clarke?'

'Probably not, sir,' Hingston replied.

'It's the same fucking story we had with the twins. No CCTV, nothing on his computer, parents haven't any fucking idea. We've searched their house and the area. We've done house to house but no material has come to light.'

Hingston's confidence in his theory that Robert Clarke had known where the twins were began to blossom, and the fact Smythe wanted to speak with him buffed up his ego some more.

'I'll give it to you, Jason, you were right to recommend we speak with Robert Clarke.'

Hingston punched the air and smiled in a way he could not if he were speaking with Smythe face to face.

Smythe continued. 'Someone in my team seems to have pissed off the Clarkes. I received a throwaway comment from Mr Clarke which suggests they have some confidence invested in *you*. I'm leaving Hounslow at five to go and see them with this bag. Can you make it?'

Hingston turned the car ignition. His clock read 4.25 p.m. 'Yes, sir.'

'Where are you?' Smythe questioned for no reason other than nosiness.

'Ealing.'

'Right. See you at five,' he reiterated and cut the call.

Smythe had parked his white 5 Series BMW at the front entrance to Hounslow Police Station. As Hingston pulled up in his Vauxhall, Smythe sauntered out of the main entrance as if the station were his stately home. He inhaled through flared nostrils and having scanned the car park which was gleaming in the June sunshine, applied a pair of Ray-Ban sunglasses. Hingston decided at this point that Smythe matched his title of DCI unequivocally; a Desperately Conceited Idiot. Smythe gave Hingston a remote acknowledgement across the car park as Hingston, inwardly smiling, locked his car and headed over to him.

On the back seat as they drove to the Clarkes' detached Victorian town house was an evidence bag which preserved the navy blue holdall suspected to belong to Daniel Clarke.

'We need to regain some confidence this evening,' Smythe stated without taking his eyes off the road. 'The press, as you've probably heard, are criticising this investigation and the Clarkes have complained that we're ineffective. A terse comment from a stressed officer has pissed them off some more.'

Hingston wondered whether the terse comment actually originated from Smythe himself, for the visit this evening was quite out of the ordinary. The Family Liaison Officer would be aware that it was taking place, but was not invited. Instead, the Senior Investigating Officer was taking Hingston, but he was officially off duty. Smythe wanted to repair the relationship with the Clarkes tonight and trusted Hingston to keep the visit to himself, otherwise they would have internal problems to deal with.

'Yes, I've been keeping up with the media reports,' Hingston confirmed.

Smythe shook his head to reinforce his frustration with allegations that evidence had been missed, insufficient resources had been allocated and that officers were poorly skilled. The local papers were, of course, unaware of the full facts of the investigation and Smythe wanted to use the remainder of the journey to get Hingston up to speed.

'Daniel's body was found at three a.m. on Friday the twentieth of May in Burlington Park. The time of death was around one thirty a.m. and as you know, he was stabbed in the neck three times. We are confident that Daniel was alone when he was attacked and that the murder was committed by one offender. The offender was left handed, believed to be taller than Daniel, strong, agile and male.'

Hingston nodded during Smythe's pause as they came to a stop at a set of traffic lights.

'This offender is a clever boy,' Smythe snorted. 'He's forensically aware which indicates?'

'The offence was planned,' Hingston responded in the manner of a good student and raised his eyebrows as he turned to look out of the passenger window.

'Precisely. Black fibres found under Daniel's fingernails and on the peripheral of one of the stab wounds suggest he fought back and that the offender ensured he was firstly, not going to leave his own DNA at the scene. Secondly, he dressed in black so that blood stains would be disguised and thirdly, to minimise the chances of being seen and subsequently identified.'

'So,' Hingston decided to show Smythe that he was capable of formulating logical hypotheses, 'are we satisfied that Daniel was lured to the park by someone he felt he could trust and that the offender was therefore also relatively young; twenty-five or under?'

'Yes, we're not suspecting the vagrant. He's probably nothing more than an old, drunken, fucking womble!' Smythe said with a smirk.

Hingston decided to remain silent and allowed Smythe to continue with his account.

'Daniel's stomach contents revealed that he had not gone without since his disappearance. He'd been living on junk food, but he'd remained healthy. It's likely that the twins had been residing with someone or some persons and yes, through trust, Daniel was lured to the park. It's possible the twins have got themselves involved in criminality be it theft, drugs, but there was no evidence from the autopsy or a search of the area to corroborate such an explanation.' Smythe took a sharp turn right, darting out in front of an oncoming vehicle. 'In respect of the forensics, the offender chose to stab Daniel on grass. He then dragged his body four metres towards a laurel bush and removed Daniel's upper clothing.'

'Okay,' Hingston acknowledged.

'He probably did this to provide a screen whilst he finished taking care of the forensics. Before leaving the scene, we believe the offender changed his footwear. Like I said, a clever boy.'

Hingston elected to pass another comment. 'So we have insufficient material to identify a suspect and that's why the Clarkes have complained we're ineffective...'

'But we now have the P.E. bag,' Smythe butted in. 'Of course we can only tell the Clarkes that we suspect this may be Daniel's bag, however, there are some marks inside that suggest it may have been used to transport items from the scene. After we've stopped at the Clarkes' we'll take a detour to get this off to the lab.'

Hingston realised that he would be spending the best part of the evening in the company of Smythe and he thought of Remi. He began to feel uncomfortable sat in Smythe's passenger seat from where he was afforded the view of his bicep stretched shirt sleeves, his tanned neck which bulged over the back of his collar and his sneering nostrils. The Ray-Bans were resting in his shirt pocket and a chunky silver chain was protruding from his right cuff.

It was officers like Smythe who bulldozed their way up the ranks. No compassion, no conscience, manipulatively deploying "friendly fire" to bring down the competition and getting fat on other officers' successes. What makes this sort of male appealing to Remi? Why the bloody hell did he take her to Will Finch's celebration drinks that Christmas? Will had joined as a probationer with Hingston, but pursued a career in Firearms. In December 2008, he moved from the Armed Response Vehicles to a Tactical Support Team and to celebrate his success, invited everyone he had ever worked with to a night out in Soho. Whilst drunk, Will chatted up Remi, who, clearly mesmerised by his snake-like coolness, gave him her number. The argument that ensued the following day when Hingston saw Will's text arrive, resulted in, as Remi put it, "some time to think" and their relationship was over. Will, at least, was a good-looking charmer. Smythe, however, the rough, selfish, bald-headed bastard... Aware the colour was rising on his neck, Hingston stared at the rush hour traffic and focused on the latest information Smythe had provided about the Clarkes.

Five minutes later, following limited further conversation, they pulled into the tree-lined avenue upon which the Clarkes' red doored residence stood. There were no press officers present because the arrest of the vagrant was not overtly connected to the Clarke case and there was no desire on the part of the police to make this public knowledge at this stage in the investigation.

* * *

Mr Clarke opened the front door and the swollen bags under his eyes shone with a plum coloured hue. Despite being the entrepreneurial owner of his own accountancy firm, his esteem and prestigious manner had drained away, leaving a brittle, tired cast of his former self.

Behind him, his nine-year-old daughter, Alice, ran up the staircase without looking back. Mrs Clarke, housewife and full-time mum, appeared in the hallway.

'Are you going to invite them in, Patrick?' she prompted quietly.

Mr Clarke stepped back from the doorway and with a limp, weary arm, directed Smythe and Hingston inside.

There were mounds of laundry and dirty plates and mugs in the kitchen. The offer of a cup of tea was declined by the officers who did not want to extend their visit.

'I understand PC Stoker has been keeping you up to date?' Smythe commenced his exchange positively. PC Stoker was the Family Liaison Officer assigned to the Clarkes.

'Yes, she's been very good throughout,' Mr Clarke spoke in a deep, sorrowful voice.

'It's a shame she's not here now,' Mrs Clarke added softly. 'She's very good with Alice.' Mrs Clarke drew a tissue from a nearby box on the cluttered kitchen island unit around which they were sat.

'But you've brought DS Hingston with you which is encouraging,' Mr Clarke commented. 'He's someone who both listens and shows diligence. Good to see you again.'

Hingston nodded.

'Yes, DS Hingston and I wanted to speak with you this evening,' Smythe said. 'I'm sure PC Stoker has done well in explaining the complexities of a police investigation and the challenges we are facing with the investigations underway.'

Mrs Clarke nodded and dabbed her nose and Mr Clarke glared at Smythe with his moist, bloodshot eyes, his pursed lips holding in his upset and his simmering anger.

Smythe repositioned himself on the bar stool to appear a little more relaxed and approachable. 'DS Hingston and I,' Smythe continued to plug the name that seemed to resonate comfortably in the Clarke household, 'are on our way to deliver an item to the forensics laboratory.'

Mr and Mrs Clarke's eyes widened in anticipation.

'Jason, step out to the car and bring in the evidence bag,' Smythe instructed as he pushed his key fob across the granite island top towards him.

Mrs Clarke's eyes moistened and she began to sniff.

As Hingston exited through the hall, Smythe continued. 'We believe we may have found the P.E. bag belonging to Daniel. If so, there is a possibility that there may be some forensic evidence…'

'About bloody time,' Mr Clarke blurted out in a wavering voice.

The front door closed and the kitchen fell quiet whilst Hingston made his way back through the hall.

Mrs Clarke climbed off her bar stool and grasped the evidence bag held by Hingston. She stretched the plastic taught across the navy blue holdall. 'This is just like Daniel's.' She blinked back tears and continued to scan the bag. 'Where did you find it?'

'More importantly,' Mr Clarke interrupted, 'have you arrested a suspect?'

'The person in possession of the bag,' Smythe spoke at a measured pace, 'does not match the offender profile. How…'

'What the…'

'Patrick!' Mrs Clarke scolded her husband.

'*However*,' Smythe continued, 'the person in possession of the bag should be able to tell us where he acquired it from. He's a vagrant and he's currently in custody sobering up having assaulted a police officer.'

'If he's assaulted a police officer, he sounds more than capable of hurting our sons!' Mr Clarke exclaimed. 'Sod your offender profiling, it's not done us any good so far!'

Mrs Clarke returned to her husband's side to try to calm him down. Hingston, having had the evidence bag released from the grip of Mrs Clarke returned to his bar stool and placed the bag on his lap.

A faint flush of colour was on Smythe's cheeks. 'Mr Clarke, we've called here this evening because the acquisition of this bag could be the turning point in this investigation. A combination of forensic evidence and an account from the vagrant could be all we need to identify the suspect.'

'Listen to the officers, Patrick,' Mrs Clarke pleaded.

'Okay,' Mr Clarke rubbed his right eyebrow. 'How long's the forensics going to take?'

'A matter of hours,' Smythe advised. He got to his feet, followed by Hingston. 'PC Stocker will update you first thing in the morning,' he assured the disquieted parents. 'We'll show ourselves out.'

Mr Clarke's emotions manifested in a deluge of tears and Mrs Clarke rubbed his heaving shoulders.

'Thank you,' she whispered.

* * *

It was nine p.m. when Hingston was dropped back off at Hounslow Police Station. The forensic scientists were busy working on the P.E. bag as well as the DNA swab and fingerprints belonging to the vagrant. Smythe was going to refuel himself at home whilst the results were awaited. Whilst he did not comment as such, Smythe was grateful that Hingston had accompanied him to the Clarkes'.

'Now, on Sunday, I expect you to make yourself present in the Major Incident Room. I'm anticipating a lot of activity over the coming days. If we secure some DNA or fingerprints, but don't get a match on the databases, then we'll be conducting intelligence led screening.'

'Okay, sir, I'll do my best to duck under the boss' radar.'

'Make sure you do that, Jason. I know Brace can be a control freak, but I outrank the old bird. Remember that,' he snorted with an arrogant sneer.

Hingston was not going to remind Smythe *again* about the condition for his return to work. Smythe had already dismissed the suggestion that there was anything wrong with him in the first place. 'I'll see you Sunday,' Hingston laughed and began to plot a plausible means of spending very little time at Chiswick Police Station on his first day back after three and a half weeks.

Chapter Seventeen
A Day of Work

Hingston had always preferred early turn shifts. At 6.31 a.m. he entered the yard at Chiswick Police Station. He hummed the melody of the musical box which he had continued to play since his night terrors came to an end a little under a week ago. From the sunlit yard he looked up at his office window on the first floor and thought back to the moment when the key dropped out of his paperwork and hit his shoe.

'Three and a half weeks,' he mused. It felt so distant. Hingston hoped that from today, the Embling-Clarke pattern could start to be broken.

On entering his office he felt as bold and polished as the mirrored capital letters which named the station on the brickwork near to the public reception. He was the first officer in and his desk was welcoming despite the absence of its usual clutter. His mug sat next to his computer and the words "Best Detective" gelled with his renewed self-worth. He skimmed his car keys onto his desk, hit the power buttons on his computer and monitor and grabbed his mug. It was teeming with mould.

'Arrghh!' he protested. 'What filthy...' and then his log in screen appeared on his monitor. He rummaged in his drawer for a Post-it note and pen and jotted down the warrant number of the person who last logged on at his desk: 193266. 'Gotcha!' he celebrated with a purposeful nod and typed in his own details to get his profile loading.

'Sarge! Good to have you back!' Rob, his DC, strode across and pulled up a swivel chair alongside Hingston.

'Good to *be* back, Rob. Here,' Hingston pushed the Post-it note towards him so that he had a direct view of the warrant number. 'Who's been using my desk?' Hingston's confidence and no-nonsense manner had returned.

'We had a personal visit from DCI Smythe on the day I phoned you about the murder. Yeah, I think that's his warrant, sarge.'

Hingston's computer had now loaded and he accessed the personnel directory. 'You're a good detective, Rob,' Hingston gave him a wink. 'He's the culprit.'

Rob gave Hingston a bemused look.

'It's almost criminal damage,' Hingston joked as he tipped the mug in Rob's direction so he had full view of the grey, white and green fuzz that was growing over the dried coffee dregs and creeping up in the direction of the rim.

'We could probably go for an ASBO,' Rob laughed.

'Morning, team,' a dominant female voice called out across the office. It was Brace, cutting short the humour and reminding them with her serious tone that there was work to be done. 'Jason,' she instructed whilst pacing her way across the grey carpet to her office. 'Give me five minutes and come in, please.'

'Yes, ma'am,' he replied.

'Shall I go and conduct a controlled explosion?' Rob held Hingston's mug at arm's-length and grinned.

'Not a bad idea,' Hingston laughed and pictured Rob walking away from the smoking remnants of Brace's office.

* * *

'Welcome back, Jason.' Brace gestured for him to sit down.

'Thank you, ma'am.'

'I have to say, Jason, I'm surprised to see you back so soon. There's a lot to be said for taking time to recover.'

Hingston stared at her tight lips which were bare of any make-up and at the absence of any crow's feet at the sides of her eyes.

She continued. 'However, I cannot argue with Occupational Health and you are clearly happy to be back. As I have said previously, I am responsible for you. That means that I don't want you overdoing it.'

Hingston wondered whether she would make specific reference to the Clarkes.

'As it happens, Brian has called in sick. He thinks he'll be back tomorrow so I propose you wait for his return before being handed responsibility for any cases, be that tomorrow or the next day. I'm sure you have a number of emails which will keep you occupied?'

'Seven hundred and sixty-two, ma'am. Popular as ever.' He threw in a charming smile.

Brace gave a slow and arrogant blink.

He seized this opportunity to set the foundation for ducking under her radar. 'I could pick up some of those emails remotely so as not to overdo it in the office?'

'That sounds sensible, Jason,' she confirmed. 'I'm pleased to see you have unwound whilst you've been away; sometimes too much enthusiasm can do more harm than good.'

'Okay, ma'am, I'll make a start here and see how it goes.'

'Manage your time according to how you feel. I'm out for a few hours this afternoon, but back by four. I don't expect to find you here when I return. *No* overtime,' she instructed.

Two hours later he was on the road to the Major Incident Room. Adrenaline was fuelling his enthusiasm to get briefed and stuck in on the case. He'd received a text from Remi last night in which she said she'd heard he was due back and that she was pleased he was better. As he drove he visualised the kiss she had added to the end of her message. Perhaps she added it in error? Or she was just being friendly, for wasn't it common for women to put kisses at the end of everything? Or... He decided to flick on the radio as a distraction.

'...Met have so far been unable to find a match for the DNA found in the school bag belonging to Daniel Clarke. Daniel was murdered on...' Hingston flicked the radio off. He gripped his steering wheel and glared ahead.

* * *

Smythe was strutting around the Major Incident Room. The activity level of the staff was high but the straight faces suggested morale was waning.

'DS Hingston!' he boomed with an air of impatience. 'You've missed the morning briefing.'

Hingston walked in the direction of Smythe. Smythe made his way through the desks towards Hingston, but had his chest out and shoulders back and appeared up for a fight.

'This was my earliest opportunity to get out of Chiswick,' Hingston explained.

'And will *Chiswick*,' Smythe applied his mocking accent once again, 'be calling you back in the next, er... ten minutes?' His words were spat with greasy sarcasm.

'I can stay for the rest of my shift, sir, unless that is no longer part of your plan?' Hingston did not care if his response sounded less than polite for neither was Smythe and technically, he should not even have been stood in the MIR.

'Right,' Smythe coughed, 'listen up.'

Hingston studied his eyes to try to predict what may come next.

'I know you keep up with the media reports, so I'm not going to repeat anything. The DNA found in the P.E. bag was Daniel's; there were blood stains and traces of grass consistent with the park so the suspect *had* used the bag to convey Daniel's bloodied clothes from the scene. The suspect's DNA has been obtained from his hair which was also in the bag. He wears it mid length and uses gel; *maybe* he used the bag to conceal a hat or mask when he left the scene. We still have not found Daniel's clothing. The vagrant is on bail,' Smythe paused to receive Hingston's nod of acknowledgement. 'He alleged that there were no items in the bag when he found it and that he'd picked it up the night before we arrested him. Conveniently, he claimed he was unable to remember where he got it from, but stated that he only acquires items from private bins and from shop refuse in Chiswick; what did I say?' Smythe curled his lip. 'A fucking womble. Officers continue to search bins but to no avail.'

'But if our suspect's forensically aware, what was he doing being so careless with the bag? The stains must have been fairly obvious.'

'There's also fingerprint evidence. The vagrant's, Daniel's and a third set, which like the DNA remains unidentified. However, the third set is only on the small handle. It is *possible* that a third party dumped the bag in a bin and *not* the key suspect, meaning there's more than one involved in this crime. Maybe it's an accomplice who's not such a clever boy. That's something we need to find out.'

'Yes, sir,' Hingston acknowledged. 'Where are we with the mass screening?'

'We're still processing samples, but we're now moving into those lower down the scoring matrix.'

'Has anyone come forward in our appeal for sightings of Robert Clarke?' Hingston was conscious that he was now questioning the Senior Investigating Officer, but it seemed that Smythe had reached a point in the investigation where he was more than content to engage in open discussion.

'No one,' Smythe growled.

'May I listen to the vagrant's interview?' Hingston asked.

'You can if you want, but it's crap.' Smythe straightened his tie as he glanced across the room.

Hingston raised his eyebrows at Smythe's unprofessional remark. Surely, that was not a reflection on the interviewing officers?

'Hostile from the off, barely cooperative even when the significance of our enquiries was explained, and I suspect, a convenient lack of memory,' added Smythe.

'What did he do to the officer at the scene?' Hingston questioned.

'Elbowed him in the stomach and kicked him in the shin causing grazing and bruising.'

'So he's up for assault but still not cooperating fully with a murder enquiry,' Hingston frowned.

'Like I said, a convenient lack of memory,' Smythe reinforced. 'Grab yourself the working copy and give me your views on it.'

* * *

Hingston sat in the pokey evidence review room. The overcrowded, buzzing IT equipment emitted a strong electrical fragrance which made the stagnant, warm air clog up Hingston's nasal passages and coat his drying mouth with a bitter film. He bounced his left leg and waited for the footage of the vagrant's interview to start. Suddenly, the salt and pepper haired, unkempt, sallow figure appeared before him. He was sat, without legal representation, like a stubborn walrus and glared at the two interviewing officers whose heads and shoulders were visible from the rear as they sat opposite him and commenced the interview.

'I am DC Holt and this is…'

'DC Browning.'

'And we are interviewing…'

'Graham Coombes,' the vagrant spoke in a tiresome tone. He sounded gruff, gravelly and had a strong Yorkshire accent.

Hingston fast-forwarded through the introductions and the caution. Smythe *had* provided an acceptable summary much to his disappointment. Graham Coombes was fond of the words "no comment" and when he did utter a response beyond the confines of these three syllables, it was to pontificate and besmirch the police force. The interview lasted forty minutes and Hingston felt short changed at its close. He made his way back to the MIR with a determined stride. Smythe was heading along the corridor and Hingston stopped him just before the gents.

'Sir. Coombes, he's staying at the hostel off Goldhawk Road?'

Smythe flared his nostrils and nodded once.

'I'll phone you if I get anything out of him,' Hingston promised with a mild glimmer of excitement in his eyes.

* * *

Graham Coombes appeared as unenthusiastic on bail as he did in the interview room. He was sat outside the hostel smoking and was in the company of a sandy-grey whippet. The June sunshine beat down on them and Coombes leaned against the rough, worn brickwork in a slovenly manner, periodically closing his eyes as if he hadn't a care in the world.

The dog's ears pricked up as Hingston approached on foot across the tarmac. She gazed at Hingston with her shiny, inquisitive eyes. She raised her eyebrows as if to question why he was looking at them and a small whimper passed from her mouth which prompted Coombes to pay attention.

Hingston's unmarked vehicle was one hundred yards down the road. However, his smart attire suggested he was on official business, either following a church service or, as Coombes suspected, representing the law.

'Allo, allo, allo!' Coombes taunted. 'I've done nowt so I suggest you find some other mug to pick on.' He did not adjust his posture and took a drag from his cigarette. Around him were numerous cigarette butts and the pasty remains of two chips and part of a burger bun which had long since been trodden into the old, craggy tarmac. The smell of stale urine rose from stained brickwork a few yards from where Coombes was leaning.

'Graham Coombes?' Hingston checked as he attempted to create an inoffensive foundation for his conversation.

'You've already interrogated me once. That's all you're getting,' Coombes replied.

'We haven't met before,' Hingston stated. 'I'm DS Hingston. I don't want you to talk to me about your arrest.'

'No concerns there. I'm saying nowt.' Coombes turned his head away from Hingston and stared down the road. He had less stubble and shorter hair since he had left custody. The hostel had provided him with the means to clean himself up to some extent. His fingernails had thick dirt underneath them and the tobacco had stained his fingers a sludgy yellow. His wiry grey eyebrows and eyelashes were dishevelled as if they had been recently rubbed and an open cold sore on his bottom lip glistened threateningly in the sunshine.

Hingston thought Coombes would not be out of place at Kallensee's Great Circus. 'How many years have you lived in Chiswick?' Hingston asked as if the question had only just occurred to him.

'Deciding if you want to move here, eh?' Coombes replied without taking his eyes off the lamp post down the road. 'More than I can count or care to remember,' he added before flicking his cigarette butt onto the tarmac. 'Might be time to move on if your lot keep harassing me, mind.' He paused. 'Once I get this piece of shit off me.' He raised the leg of his jeans to reveal the tracking device which was fixed to his ankle.

Hingston suspected Coombes was about to launch into a session of hurling false allegations against the police, so he decided to cut to the chase. 'I believe you know this area very well. I also believe you can help with an enquiry which could save the lives of two boys.'

Coombes showed no signs of engaging. 'Should never 'ave taken that bag,' Coombes protested unexpectedly.

'I'm not interested in the bag,' Hingston insisted.

Coombes glanced at Hingston distrustfully with his amber eyes, but remained silent.

'I believe you may have seen this boy.' Hingston held a photograph of Robert Clarke towards him.

'You believe a lot but know nowt,' Coombes huffed without looking.

'Just *look* at the photo,' Hingston instructed.

The whippet obliged and with a scratching of claws on the tarmac, came over to Hingston.

'Bleedin' dog!' Coombes complained. 'Told you we don't like policemen.' He glanced up at the photograph, his curiosity having got the better of him. Hingston watched his eyes widen before he looked at the dog and changed the subject. 'You gonna leave me in peace or are you just trying to find another reason to arrest me?'

'I'm not here to arrest you. I'm asking you to tell me where and when you saw this boy.'

'What's in it for me?'

'There's a family who have lost their three sons. One has been murdered and two remain missing. Apart from helping them, to assist in this enquiry may go in your favour at court.'

Coombes called the dog back to him and Hingston waited for his reply.

'I *have* seen that kid,' he affirmed.

Hingston stood still, an eruption of jubilation being contained and disguised.

'It was a couple of streets off the back of Burlington Park.'

Hingston's heart was racing. 'Tell me more,' he prompted.

Chapter Eighteen
Operation PANDORA

At 4.28 the next morning, all was silent. A further eighteen minutes would pass before sunrise, a further two before a gentle clunk would stir the starlings on Cranbrook Avenue, Chiswick.

In Hatch End, Hingston lay on his bed awake and in thought. Operation PANDORA was in progress; an unmatchable surge of coordinated activity had been sustained for sixteen hours and now, for the next two minutes, there would be a calm, reinforcement of duties and objectives before Cranbrook Avenue would receive its covert crusaders.

Hingston watched the red digits on his alarm clock blink to Burlington Bertie, an apt piece of bingo slang for the time which would hopefully see the capture of Daniel Clarke's murderer who committed his crime in Burlington Park.

The riot vehicle was parked fifty yards down from number 46 Cranbrook Avenue. With his hand on the latch of the van's rear door, the sergeant spoke over his Airwave terminal to the Control Room to confirm his unit were ready to be deployed from the vehicle. He eased the door open with a gentle clunk and in a low voice urged his unit to follow their orders. 'Go, go, go!'

They exited with the coordination and nimbleness of a dance troupe and with the stealth of an army of giant black ants with size thirteen feet. Along the pavement they hurried with the neighbourhood asleep and as unaware of their presence as they would be of overnight snowfall.

Number 46 had no gate which enabled swift access to the front door. Intelligence checks and covert surveillance earlier that night indicated that this rental property was being sublet to a twenty-two-year-old named Raymond Johnson whose associates included two suspected drug dealers, one of whom, a twenty-four-year-old named Ryan Dix, was seen entering the property at one a.m. this morning. It was this information which added credibility to Coombes' account.

Coombes' evidence was limited but coherent. Having found himself "robbed" of his remaining small change by "a homeless bastard" he was unable to purchase any drink. As a result, he had an afternoon of sobriety on Saturday the 28th of May, during which time he took to rummaging in the refuse bins behind Burlington Park. He later found himself on Cranbrook Avenue and noticed a boy in his early teens "scurrying about with the look of a demented rabbit". He watched the boy, now identified by Coombes as Robert Clarke, inspect the numbers on the brick posts and front doors before reaching a house that was missing its entrance gate and which had a navy gloss painted door. Coombes watched Robert pause, "look about like he were up t'som'int", ring the doorbell and wait. During this time Robert approached the bay window and tried to squint through the nets. The front door was opened by an obese twenty-something-year-old who was tattooed. He stepped back into the hall and Robert stepped up to the door frame, at which point he was pulled inside by his shoulder and the door was shut. The obese man matched the profile of Ryan Dix. Dix was a troublemaker and had recently been suspected of dealing in cannabis, but insufficient evidence had prevented an arrest.

Now, the parts played by Dix and Johnson in the Clarke case were about to be exposed.

Crouched beside the low brick wall of 46 Cranbrook Avenue, the tactical team in their black boiler suits and body armour waited in silence. The sergeant had placed himself two officers from the head of this bulky, testosterone charged line and peered discretely over the wall at the poorly maintained semi-detached house. The lights were off and the curtains were drawn. He ducked back behind the wall and placed a strong grip on the left shoulder of the officer in front of him. 'Go!' he ordered in a hushed voice.

The two lead officers rose and proceeded up the concrete path to the navy front door. One stepped to the side whilst the other swung the heavy, red painted battering ram backwards and with a fast swing, plunged its weight into the door. A tremendous thud signalled the remaining officers to charge up the path and storm into the hallway past the broken door which had been ripped off its frame in one manoeuvre. Choreographed to perfection, each officer infiltrated a different part of the house; one to the front room, one to the kitchen, one to the back room, one guarded the hall and numerous ran upstairs. All were armed and all filled the semi with the boisterous and domineering call of 'Police!'

Upon a threadbare chocolate brown sofa, a terrified youth, shaken from his sleep, threw his hands behind his head American-style and stared at the officers with bloodshot, bulging eyes. The youth began whimpering and his pale blue jogging bottoms developed a rapidly expanding dark patch. He had been asleep in his hoody and there was a pizza stain on it. Around the sofa were open cans of lager, a couple of which had been knocked over the day before and a strong, stale stench stagnated in the air. There was evidence of an evening of drug taking; littered on the sofa and the floor were Rizla papers, lighters and disused small square sachets which contained traces of weed.

The footsteps overhead were heavy and the youth jumped when a horrendous crash shook the ceiling above. Officers had broken down the door to the bathroom. Ryan Dix had locked himself inside, having escaped his bedroom seconds before the police entered the upstairs hallway. The toilet had been flushed and the cistern was refilling. Dix stood there smirking as he was arrested. He had succeeded in destroying whatever drugs had been in his possession and his smugness was as slimy as the stains in the toilet pan.

Whilst Dix was cuffed by two officers, his huge torso making it difficult to pull his tattooed, flabby arms behind him, another officer noticed the bathroom window was ajar. He pushed it open and saw Raymond Johnson on the flat roof, trying to prepare for a long jump over the fence into the neighbour's garden.

'Stop! Police!' the officer yelled.

Johnson, horrified, made his jump and wailed 'fuck you pigs!' whilst mid-air.

The officer in the kitchen burst out into the garden in pursuit. Johnson had just skimmed the fence and was now in the garden next door. The officer scaled the fence and discovered Johnson clutching his ankle and cursing. He was doubled over on the patio and spat at the officer, despite his attempts to check on the youth's condition.

Meanwhile, in the front room, the urine-stained "hoody" was becoming more anxious. 'I ain't done nothin', d'ya understand what I'm sayin'?' he squeaked.

The sergeant could be heard in the hallway updating the Control Room. 'Three males: Ryan Dix, Raymond Johnson and an unidentified male. The Clarkes are not present. Repeat, *not* present.'

The hoody began to shake. 'I'm not involved in dat fuck up.'

'Sarge!' the officer called.

'You wan dem, you gotta look elsewhere. Try Shaze's.'

The sergeant entered the room, stood alongside his officer and glared down at the pitiful wreck on the sofa whose bulging eyes were welling up.

'Dixie's gonna kill me,' the hoody whined.

'The kid's told us to look at Shaze's for the Clarkes.'

'Who's Shaze?' the sergeant directed his question at the hoody.

The hoody was crying and pulling at his hair.

The sergeant spoke over his radio to the Control Room. 'Intel check, please; Shaze.' He walked up to the hoody. 'Where does Shaze live?'

'Next door ta Dix,' he snorted and cuffed the glutinous mucous which was hanging from both nostrils. 'Shepherd's Bush.'

The Control Room had a match for Shaze. 'We've got a Shane Dobbs, one eight seven Angel Road, Shepherd's Bush. Convicted burglar. Last offence two thousand and two. We've got a unit on location already, waiting to enter one eight nine Angel Road, the home address of Ryan Dix.'

'Advise the SIO we've received intel the Clarkes are with Shane Dobbs.'

'Now I've helped ya, I'm in da clear, right?' the panicked hoody begged through his drying tears.

He received no reply.

Three minutes later, moments before sunrise, the occupants of 187 Angel Road received an equally well rehearsed explosion of uninvited visitors. As the officers surged into the building, a further tactical unit arrived for back up.

Numerous rooms made up 187 Angel Road; it was a larger property than 46 Cranbrook Avenue and Shaze appeared to be housing persons with unusual sleeping patterns, for three of the front windows were lit at quarter to five in the morning. The officers barged their way into every room and found Shaze, who had been asleep with a naked woman, on the second floor.

The clamour of swearing and shouting throughout the house took several minutes to subside. A few rooms were empty, but most housed evidence of a brothel. Instead of breaking into other people's houses to steal, Shaze had opened up his own to desperate women who he could exploit sexually and financially, carrying out his crimes under the guise of an everyday supermarket employee.

As Shaze was ordered out of bed, he reached for a pair of burgundy red boxer shorts. Beneath them lay a striped navy and gold piece of fabric. The officer strode over and discovered it to be a school tie, the colours of the Clarkes' school.

Footsteps thundered up the staircase. 'They're in the basement in a poor state. He's imprisoned them,' a blue-eyed officer stared at Shaze.

* * *

The ivory bed linen felt soap-sud soft as Hingston reached across his duvet and placed his fingers on the winding key. Unbeknown to him as he wound the mechanism of the musical box, the activity on Angel Road was peaking.

Two ambulances hurtled along the Uxbridge Road in response to a call for medical assistance fired to the Control Room. When they arrived on Angel Road a swathe of police cars were parked outside Shaze's property filling the gap between the two riot vehicles and containing the occupants on the pavement in front of the house. Neighbours were drawn to their windows, porches and in some instances, into the street.

The paramedics in bottle green were provided immediate access to the basement where Nathan and Robert Clarke had been found gagged and bound on the dirt-ridden, hard, stone floor. The boys had been kept alive, but they had been drugged and their condition was poor. As they were lifted upon stretchers, the handcuffed offenders split between Angel Road and Cranbrook Avenue were escorted into individual police cars and swept off to a number of the Met's custody suites.

Whilst the blue and red lights spun silently above the silver vehicles on their rapid journeys away from the scenes, Hingston's bedroom filled with the glorious sound of the musical box.

Two further addresses in Shepherd's Bush and Hackney were raided by police minutes later, adding a further three persons to the arrest count. Whilst the custody suites received and booked in the suspects, a search of the properties commenced and the Clarkes were finally reunited at Ealing Hospital.

Soon after six a.m. Hingston arrived at the Major Incident Room. Brace was expecting him at Chiswick for seven, but he brushed that requirement aside. He needed to know whether his reinvestigation of the Emblings' case had enabled him to save the Clarkes and whether any more parallels were coming to light.

Chapter Nineteen
One Ring on the Oak Tree

Dear Detective Sergeant Hingston,

It is with immense pleasure and anticipation that I write to you following receipt of your most intriguing letter dated the 20th of October 2012. I hasten to add that you are welcome to visit soonest and of course at a time convenient to yourself.

As the great-grandson of Neville Embling, youngest sibling of the twins, I feel both astonished and honoured to be receiving, for my family, some closure on this sad tragedy.

Whilst Neville was too young to have formed many memories of his dear brothers, he did of course pass down the generations the account of the untimely fate of Charles and the loss of George and John, to which countless possibilities and numerous heart wrenching conclusions have been debated over the years by my family. As you know, this is the first contact we have had with the police since 1867 and we are most grateful you have made the effort to find us all these generations on.

It is apparent you have devoted a great deal of your time and interest in unearthing some of the truths of the past, which I am amazed and somewhat touched to hear have also assisted in a present day police investigation.

In exchange for your kindness, I have searched the family archives and located an item or two which I am sure will be of interest to you. I look forward to sharing these with you when we meet and thank you for contacting me.

Yours sincerely,
Peter Embling

Chapter Twenty
A Finale for the Beginning

The journey from Hatch End to Bristol on this bright November morning had provided Hingston with ample time to consider the events of the past year and a half.

The success of Operation PANDORA exposed more criminality than the police had anticipated and for Hingston, revealed more evidence to strengthen the Embling-Clarke pattern. After an intense, protracted investigation and trial at the Old Bailey which concluded a little under two months ago, the facts were finally clear.

Daniel and Nathan Clarke had been out on their morning paper round in May 2010 when the occupant of a maisonette came to his door. The occupant was Raymond Johnson who subsequently moved to Cranbrook Avenue in early 2011. Johnson asked the twins if they would take a package to an address a few roads away and offered them £10. The twins jumped at this opportunity to increase their week's earnings by almost fifty percent. Johnson appeared again a fortnight later with a similar request. Very soon the twins were regularly couriering packages for him; all of which, unbeknown to them at the outset, contained drugs.

Johnson was a member of a gang which formed in 2009. He and Ryan Dix had brought a number of friends from Chiswick and Shepherd's Bush together; some a worse influence than others and most of whom were in their late teens. Dix, being the largest and the eldest, became the gang leader.

Dix also had a personal "business arrangement" with his next door neighbour, Shaze, in Angel Road: he supplied Shaze with cannabis in exchange for sexual favours from the prostitutes Shaze pimped.

Shaze had stacked shelves at a local supermarket after serving a prison sentence for burglary in 2002. His objective was to remain off the police radar so that he could secretly manage a brothel and he had done this successfully for a number of years. There was no intelligence to link him to Dix until the hoody's outburst on the morning of the 6th of June.

Dix remained the leader of the gang until early 2011 when he unwisely brought in a new associate; a twenty-three-year-old drug dealer, unknown to police, named Max Burrows.

Burrows lived in Hackney and it was his address that was also raided by police on the morning of the 6th of June 2011. Burrows was sullen and had a venomous streak. He soon took control of the gang, pushing Dix into second place. He manipulated them all with the drugs to which they had become addicted. He often did so from afar in Hackney, but ensured he remained kingpin by crashing down at their addresses in Chiswick and Shepherd's Bush unexpectedly, boasting, demanding and belittling those around him whilst feeding their drug dependencies.

Before long, Burrows had his drug-washed eyes fixed on Shaze and his girls; the shadows that hung beneath Burrows' eyes created a thick fog behind which misogynistic meditations festered.

Nathan Clarke admitted during his police interview that he and Daniel had lied to their parents on a number of occasions, where instead of studying or spending time at the local park they were associating with the gang.

On the afternoon of Friday the 15th of April 2011, the Clarke twins had been invited to Cranbrook Avenue for a party. They had been told by Johnson that they had to get there straight after school, because some girls were coming round and if they want some action as pee wees they've got to earn it first. Nathan Clarke stressed to the police that he and Daniel were not going to take up the offer of the girls, but wanted to remain part of the gang. On reflection, Nathan formed the opinion that they were just being used, but at the time they felt "liked" and they found the gang and the money "exciting".

Burrows attended the party and gave the twins an ultimatum: "Piss off home now, tell mummy and daddy you were being naughty little school boys and have nothing more to do with us, or stay until *I tell you* you can leave and prove you're part of this gang." The twins chose to stay.

Nathan explained that once they had stayed one night it was harder to leave; they were going to get in more trouble at home and the longer they stayed the more respect they were getting from the gang. Burrows and Dix fed the twins' fear of the consequences of involving the police and the gang applied increasing peer pressure to make them stay. Combined, their actions outweighed and suffocated the twins' immature consciences.

The days continued to roll by and according to Nathan, he and Daniel spent time packaging small quantities of drugs at Cranbrook Avenue where they played computer games, associated with the gang and did whatever they were asked to do indoors.

The night before Daniel was murdered there was yet another party at the house. Some girls from Angel Road came round accompanied by Burrows and Dix. In the early hours of the morning, Nathan left the main party downstairs to go to the bathroom. The door to the bedroom adjoining the bathroom was ajar and the light was off. He heard a girl crying and pushed the door open, flooding the scene with light from the hall.

Upon the dishevelled duvet was one of Shaze's girls. She looked much younger than the rest, no more than sixteen and her face was sickly pale in the light. Down her cheeks mascara ran and mingled with crimson blood which stemmed from her eyebrow. Her scream which followed filled the bedroom but was lost to the rest of the house by the booming dance music that pulsated up through the hallway. She stretched her arm toward Nathan who stood aghast and looked into her wide, helpless eyes.

Burrows sauntered into view, topless, holding his belt and faced Nathan; his dish plate pupils were framed by the dark shadows of his demented eyes. "There's nothing to see, *Daniel*", Burrows hissed as Nathan hurled himself at the bony monster and yelled to the girl to "get out!".

Nathan explained to police that the girl ran out of the room as he fought with Burrows and that very soon after he was thrown to the floor and lost consciousness.

The next night, Dix told Daniel that Burrows wanted him to take some drugs to Burlington Park; it was to be his first deal.

Nathan regretted his failure to tell Daniel about what happened at the party. It took an extended period of crying before he could tell police it was due to mistaken identity that Daniel was murdered and that he wished they had not been identical twins.

The criminal investigation proved Nathan's belief that Burrows murdered Daniel believing he was the twin who interrupted his attack on the girl.

The similarity between the scene which played out in the present day bedroom and the actions of the Victorian, bearded red-head toward the terrified Circassian girl astonished Hingston. He concluded that history *had* somehow repeated itself. When Charles Embling was murdered, he most probably too was mistaken for his twin. In which case, it was George who came to the rescue of the Circassian girl.

Unlike the red-head who escaped justice, Burrows *was* convicted of Daniel's murder. Burrows attributed blame to "the kid showin' me disrespect". It was his DNA which was found inside the P.E. bag. The fingerprints on the handle of the bag belonged to Dix who had carelessly discarded the empty bag in a nearby residential street. He was also convicted of a charge of conspiracy to murder and sentenced to a minimum of fifteen years in prison. The murder weapon was not found, however, Dix alleged Burrows disposed of it in the Thames.

Shaze found himself back in prison for perverting the course of justice, false imprisonment, rape and for running a brothel. Shaze alleged that he allowed his basement to be used to imprison the Clarkes because Burrows was blackmailing him. However, the investigation revealed that he was actually receiving payment from Burrows to do so and that he split the payment with Dix who had proposed the business arrangement.

The hoody who blew the whistle on Shaze and in turn on Dix and Burrows, did not escape without convictions of perverting the course of justice and of drug offences. Johnson and another three members of the gang were similarly convicted. Combined, all offenders in the Clarke case were sentenced to a minimum of seventy-nine years in prison.

Both Nathan and Robert continued to receive counselling sixteen months after they were rescued from Angel Road. The answer as to how Robert Clarke knew where he may find his brothers was simple. He had overheard the twins talk of Johnson and in early 2011 had followed them to Cranbrook Avenue on his bike. For reasons which may never be understood, he decided to find Nathan on his own without involving his parents or the police.

The vagrant, Graham Coombes, and his whippet, relocated back to Yorkshire to live with his brother where he planned to make a fresh start.

Following the trial, Hingston was praised for his "investigative excellence and tenacity" by Smythe who broadcast the success of

Operation PANDORA at every opportunity. Smythe, in his usual bombastic manner, did of course ensure that each time he credited *himself* with a bit more praise, and each time he did so in a slightly *louder voice* than he did for Hingston. However, recognition of Hingston's success was not going to be forgotten, especially by Mr and Mrs Clarke. They wrote a letter of gratitude to Hingston for saving the lives of two of their three boys, which they addressed for the attention of Brace.

Brace did, with a degree of effort, muster a smile for Hingston's contribution to the murder investigation and reminded him that his purposeful disregard for the conditions set by Occupational Health was not to be repeated under any circumstances. The ultimate safety of Nathan and Robert Clarke excused him – just about.

Uncle Zack and Remi were both delighted with the outcome. Zack, with his sporting enthusiasm, gave Hingston a pep talk on climbing the ranks and "showing Brace how to be a DI". Remi, blinking her eyes enthusiastically, suggested to Hingston he should transfer to the murder squad at the earliest opportunity. To Hingston's great pleasure, she acknowledged that Smythe had become a little puffed up and irritating following Op PANDORA and his attitude disappointed her.

Now, on this brisk November morning, Hingston's polished Oxfords tapped on the smooth granite steps which led to the large, olive green front door. He allowed himself a moment to inhale the scent of an applewood bonfire which had sweetly infused the chilled air and he admired the rich, red ivy which enrobed High Oaks House, the Georgian residence owned by Peter Embling. Today's meeting with Peter would provide the Embling family with a long overdue conclusion to the tragic events of 1866. Peter's promise of an item or two of information from the Embling family archives filled Hingston with anticipation. He reached toward the ornate, brass lion head door knocker and the door opened unexpectedly.

'Detective Sergeant Hingston! Welcome!' A broad smile and outstretched arm beckoned him inside. 'I do hope you don't consider me a silly old fool greeting you in such an excited manner, but I've been counting down the days like a schoolboy waiting for Christmas!' Peter Embling was jovial and spritely for a gentleman of eighty-one. His blue eyes glistened and his hand trembled as he firmly shook Hingston's, clasping his left over the top in the style of a long lost relative.

'Not at all, Mr Embling. It's my pleasure to meet you,' Hingston smiled. He scanned the hallway noting the traditional decor, the family photographs, the antique telephone and the sweeping staircase.

'Do come; follow me through into the lounge.' Peter Embling led the way much like he were Hingston's grandfather. 'I had my daughter bake us a cake.'

The pair sat down opposite each other on the grand sofas with their slices of Victoria sponge and cups of tea resting on the table between them. An open fire crackled and spat embers.

'Now, down to business. Tell me more about your detective findings!' Peter encouraged.

'I must emphasise,' Hingston looked Peter straight in the eye, 'my investigation into Charles and George *could not* have commenced without the amazing discoveries of a small key and its musical box.' Hingston reached deep into the sturdy bag he had carried with him and lifted out his prized possession wrapped in a soft blanket. 'I will play it at the end as my finale.' Hingston placed it on the coffee table. He spoke frankly, describing to Peter Embling each step of his investigation into the past and touched upon his personal difficulties which in hindsight were crucial to solving both cases.

197

'Well, Detective Sergeant, it is satisfying to finally know *why* Charles and George left home and quite astonishing that young John managed to navigate his way to Cadbury; what a feat for someone so small and unequipped. And what a brave boy was our George. I do believe your deduction to be correct there, Detective Sergeant. I feel the need to voice my utmost *distaste* for the evil creature that took the life of Charles and framed that poor woman. And I will always continue to wonder what became of George and John, but alas, that we shall never know.'

Hingston gave Peter a solemn nod of recognition. 'There remains one name which I've been unable to place. *Jasper*.'

'Good lord!' Peter exclaimed.

An old travel case sat next to Peter on the sofa. With a knowing smile he glanced at Hingston and opened the lid. 'Here is a photographic portrait of the family taken under a year before the twins left.' Peter rose from his seat and joined Hingston. 'Look. There is Charles and George. I cannot tell you which is which. See the curly hair. Both blond ringlets.'

Hingston stared at the worn photograph, the familiarity striking an emotional chord. Their faces, seen for the first time, appeared handsome, gentle and refined. Viewing the whole family together saddened Hingston. He remembered the embroidered names on Elizabeth Embling's handkerchief. They were now so real.

'There is John,' Peter pointed with a finger which wavered by John's boots, 'and stood next to him is my great-grandfather, Neville.' He moved the photograph into Hingston's hand and continued to name the siblings and their parents.

Hingston sat in silence, familiarising himself with the scene. Their expressions were calm and serious as in any Victorian photograph, peaceful and unaware of their futures. He stared at each of them, memorising their features which previously he had only been able to imagine.

Peter reached across the photograph and pointed. 'And on the end, Jasper.'

His question was now answered. Jasper was a spaniel. The family pet. Hingston laughed and shook his head. 'At last. Mystery solved!'

'Well... you don't know what I'm about to take out of this case next, detective.'

Hingston's heart began to race.

'Here is the journal kept by my great-great-grandfather. That, as you know, is Richard Embling, father of the twins.' He passed the journal to Hingston. 'I knew you would want to see this and I've had a typed transcript produced so that you can take a copy away with you and also a copy of the photograph.'

Hingston sat still and pale.

'It's a sad read overall. You will see that he wrote periodically. More so after the boys had gone. His feelings are well restrained as you would expect of that era. However, this is where you will discover some home truths shall we say; some facts which would otherwise have been lost. And if I may draw your attention to this entry,' he reached to the journal and turned to the bookmarked page, 'scribed on the thirteenth of March eighteen sixty-eight.'

"Elizabeth has taken to the bedroom, feverish and forlorn. Their possessions she disposed of yesterday, clothes, remaining toys and the musical box, much to my protestations. The musical box had been locked prior to their departure from our lives. The key either taken by the twins who loved the music so dearly or hidden somewhere we cannot find. Whichever does apply, my sons and their music are gone but live on in my memory."

Hingston's eyes prickled as he read and reread Richard Embling's words.

'You see, Detective Hingston, the key had been separated from its box prior to October eighteen sixty-six. There was only one key.

How it found itself within your crime file not far short of one hundred and fifty years later is well beyond our understanding.'

Hingston held the journal by its leather cover, moving his fingers against the grain as he gazed down at Richard Embling's confessions.

Peter continued. 'As you read on, the journal reveals that Elizabeth slipped further into depression and into what was diagnosed as hysteria. Her system became so weak that when she became infected with scarlatina in eighteen sixty-nine she sadly died before the New Year.'

Hingston pictured Richard Embling sat at an elegant writing desk, scribing his lamentations across the velum pages. There were only momentary pauses, evident from darker strokes created when extra ink was absorbed mid-sentence. He wondered just how much resilience was required to comprehend such tragedies and maintain composure. Patrick Clarke had not managed the situation so well when his family was thrown into turmoil. Indeed, through the Emblings' tragedy, the Clarkes were saved from the loss of two further sons and the unthinkable crisis that would have followed.

Hingston lifted his head and met Peter Embling's warm eyes. 'I'm sorry for Richard Embling's loss. I can't imagine how he coped on his own with the three remaining children after such a series of tragedies.'

'He did so very well according to my great-grandfather. This is a woeful tale and his journal will hit you hard emotionally. However, it's important you remember that this shaped my family's future. Richard Embling ultimately provided funding for an orphanage that was managed by Neville and subsequently my grandfather. For sixty years that orphanage served hundreds of children very well. I shan't hesitate to say that had it not been for those family tragedies, that orphanage would never have existed. You have to look for the positives in such situations. Detective

Hingston, if you do not mind me being forward in my observations?'

'No, of course not.'

'What is clear to me, is that you have delivered the same first class service to my relatives' case as you do in your day job. And, most importantly, you have delivered justice. The woman who was hanged for murder, Miss…'

'Miss Tolcher,' Hingston prompted.

'…has been exonerated,' Peter said.

Hingston continued. 'And by ascertaining that she sighted John in Cadbury led to my pursuit of the vagrant who, like Miss Tolcher, was questioned by police and who coincidently had, in a similar way, sighted the twins' brother. If only the Victorian police had asked Miss Tolcher about John Embling.'

'You shouldn't feel sad about the past,' Peter stressed, 'because you cannot return and change it. You should focus on the justice you have delivered. What was wrong is now right. It is clear to me that *you* were the only one who could stop history repeating itself. That is why you experienced the night terrors. That is why the key and the musical box found their way to you.'

'Thank you.' Hingston shook Peter's hand. 'Your words have touched me. I mean that sincerely. Thank you.'

'My pleasure, Detective Sergeant.'

The embers in the fireplace popped as Hingston gathered his thoughts. He raised his eyebrows, about to speak, but his words were halted by a sudden burst of activity on the drive at the front of High Oaks House.

A child's laughter carried on the cool November air and hurried footsteps scrunched and slipped in the gravel.

Hingston turned to look out of the window.

'Who on earth is that?' Peter said.

His reply chilled Hingston. He could see no one. Memories of the churchyard in Newton St Cyres flooded back to him and he rose to his feet.

The commotion continued and Hingston rushed to the front door. Peter headed towards the window to watch.

Hingston stepped out onto the granite steps and into silence. The deep, swept gravel was untouched except for the trail left by Hingston's car tyres and his own footmarks up to the house. He scanned the property and realised that the sweet smell of the bonfire had been replaced with the perfume of honeysuckle. He felt nervous for the first time since May last year.

On his car windscreen, he noticed a piece of paper, small and brown, clipped under one of the wipers. He ran across the gravel. As he eased the paper free, he turned back to the house. Peter was now watching from the open front door.

'It appears to be a note,' Hingston called, scanning the empty drive. He hurried back to the warmth of the house.

The pair stood quietly as Hingston opened the unmarked paper which enclosed two items – a newspaper cutting headed "Circus Death Horror" and a small, worn photograph. He felt sick. The photograph slipped from his fingers as he read the report of the demise of the Circassian girl's father. The death occurred on the 27th of May 1866, only months before the Embling twins joined the circus.

Hingston looked at Peter Embling who was stood next to him. He had picked up the photograph and was frowning at it.

'What is it?' Hingston asked.

Peter handed him the photograph without passing comment.

Hingston stared at the blond man who was stood with the beautiful Circassian girl outside a tent, presumably one of those belonging to Kallensee's Great Circus. Her scarlet lips were a dark sepia.

'It's remarkable,' said Peter. 'Who are they?'

'They're circus performers.' Hingston looked Peter in the eye to gauge his reaction.

'But… give him dark hair… and he looks, well, just like *you*,' Peter said.

Hingston flipped the photograph over and read the words: "To the one I can rely upon, with love". He suggested they return to the lounge and closed the front door, taking one last look across the drive.

They found little to say as they drank their tea, looking at the newspaper and the photograph. For Hingston, a new set of questions emerged.

Peter spoke. 'You were about to say something earlier…'

'Yes, I was,' smiled Hingston, looking at Peter and glancing at the musical box.

The honey coloured grain glowed with a delicate gold hue and as he watched, the gentle sway of the meadow began to drift back and forth across its pattern. In a miniature field on the lid of the box, the curly haired boy ran once more. He ran through the silky eared grasses; the summer-soft evening sunshine radiated on him and in the distance was a figure. Hingston stared at the horizon. He was mistaken! There were two figures. The boy ran faster and bounced towards them, waving both hands in the air. They ran towards him and with their arms outstretched, they came clearly into view. Into the open arms of his twin and the Circassian girl he fell. They were reunited. Hingston could not take his eyes away from the scene of childhood elation. The Circassian girl then raised one of her hands and she waved it back and forth with a casual and familiar twist of her wrist and looked happily into Hingston's eyes.

Hingston gazed back at her beautiful smile and realised her eyes were charged with energy. In a fleeting moment which chilled his mind with the same trickery as déjà vu, Hingston pictured the elderly woman stood in the meadow, waving in the same way. He heard her words: "maybe it was my time to do something in return" and was engulfed by the strangest mix of emotions. Distracting him from his thoughts, the trio were joined by the young John and their spaniel, Jasper, and the scene melted into the grain of the wood.

Hingston turned to Peter who appeared not to have noticed his momentary silence. 'Please, let me play the musical box.' Hingston smiled with a flush of realisation radiating from his chest. 'As I said, the finale. I'm hoping you may be able to tell me the name of the tune for there isn't a card inside the box.' He wound the key, replaying in his mind the images of the meadow. And there was the familiar lilting melody, rising and falling with rich glissandos. Hingston allowed it to play to its natural end and turned to Peter.

'Well! Again, you have asked the right person,' Peter chuckled. 'The tune in question is from an operetta written by Vincenzo Bellini; it's about a Druid priestess named Norma.'

Hingston's eyes sparkled.

'The title of the tune is "Mira, o Norma", or in English, "Hear Me, Norma".'

'Norma?' said Hingston. '"Hear Me, Norma"!' He broke into gentle laughter. A tear came to his eye. 'Norma was Miss Eliza Tolcher's middle name *and* she was a Druid!'

'Well, I think that's an apt finale, Detective Sergeant. I wouldn't be at all surprised if Norma has been listening to you all along.'

* * *

Through clouds of sadness
The sun of joy appears
How bright the gladness
That shineth thro' our tears

Hear Me, Norma – The Celebrated Duet
Charles Jefferys. Lyricist. (1807-1865)